To Elaine (aka laneyloo),
Without her help and inspiration this
book would not have been possible.

SQUIRREL APOCALYPSE
GOLGOTHA
THE PLACE OF SKULLS

SQUIRREL APOCALYPSE
GOLGOTHA

◆ ◆ ◆

THE PLACE OF SKULLS

by Smylie James

T rying to cross Liverpool Bay in the middle of the night on tiny rafts made of old plastic bottles lashed together with bits of string, was surely an act of madness.

This madness was born out of desperation. The Red Squirrel population of Anglesey, once numbered in their thousands now reduced to less than a hundred, the result of a vicious war with the invading Grey Squirrels from the mainland, their only choice was to push their tiny crafts out into the sea, hoping the currents would carry them across the bay to the promised land of Formby, where they could find safety and a new life.

The break of day on Formby beach revealed the heart-rending sight of an armada of tiny rafts being thrown onto the beach by the incoming tide. Many that had survived the perilous crossing of Liverpool Bay, now succumbed to the swirling surf, their little bodies rigid in death; others were pitched cruelly on to the sands by the merciless tide, their coats once so vividly red now bleached grey by the saltwater.

Some bravely defying the elements had fought their way ashore, these lucky ones now huddled together in the mountainous sand dunes that loomed over the beach, shivering and shaking from their ordeal the recriminations had begun, angry mutterings now given loud voice –

'Madness, absolute madness, I told you we should never have left Anglesey, we would have been better off taking our chances with the Greys.'

Any further discord cut short by the sudden appearance from the sand dunes of a large party of heavily armed Red Squirrels, their leader, conspicuous by only having one ear, barked out the order.

'On your knees now, paws on your heads all of you.'

This was not the welcome the little band of refugees were hoping for, but exhausted by the journey, they meekly obeyed. Striding forward the one-eared squirrel addressed them.

'I am Olaf Nutter the Commander of the Viking Division of the armed forces of the Squirrel Republic of Formby, by invading our territory you have committed the ultimate crime, there is only one punishment for this crime - DEATH! Will you Greys never learn?'

The wail of anguish was palpable.

'Sir please may I speak' said one of the refugees, the desperation of the situation made him reckless.

'We are not invaders but Reds like you, we are your brothers from the Island of Anglesey driven from our homes by the Greys, look, the salt has stained our coats.'

With that he franticly began rubbing at his coat to reveal the red under the salt stains. Commander Nutter was not impressed.

'Well brother, even if what you say is true, you have violated our strict quarantine laws; you will be placed in an isolation camp, examined by our medical staff, any of you found to be sick will be returned to the sea on the next tide, the rest, male and female, will be conscripted into our defence forces; we, in the Viking Republic of Formby, do not tolerate immigration of any kind.'

'Take them away and make sure there is no physical contact until they have been examined by the medics, burn all their possessions except their boats, they might be needing those.'

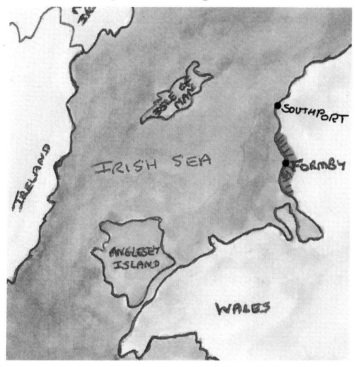

THE PROMISED LAND

So this was the promised land of Formby that our little band of travellers had braved the perils of The Irish Sea to reach!

No land of milk and honey but a paranoid one-party state, led by the personality cult of the Supreme Leader, Kemel Red, a 33rd direct descendant of the Republic's founder Atta-Tac-Red. Where he came from was shrouded by myth and legend: A fearsome fighter, his very name derived from his inability to pronounce his trade mark battle cry "attack," due to an agonising stammer made worse by his abnormally large front teeth, a trait which all his subsequent descendants would inherit, along with jet black tails and black ear tufts which marked them out from other squirrels.

When Atta-Tac-Red's raft was swept onto Formby sands, he and his family had been on their way to Anglesey, fleeing the Isle of Man after an abortive attempt to take over the colony there had gone spectacularly wrong.

The strong currents in Liverpool Bay had forced them ashore at Formby, where they found giant pine trees and an abundance of pine cones; in short, an ideal place to start a new life; only one problem, there was already a Red Squirrel population living in Formby and it was not about to give up its home to the newcomers.

A meeting was convened with the local Red Squirrel leadership. At this meeting Atta-Tac-Red offered his daughter Rougina in marriage to Nutkin-the-Fat, the self-styled "Squirrel King" of Formby.

Nutkin an odious creature despised by his own kind could hardly contain himself, the prospect of marriage to such a spellbinding beauty as Rougina totally clouded his judgement, and he proposed a great feast to celebrate the proposed marriage.

Atta-Tac-Red produced a special barrel of Cone Nip Pinecone Brandy that he had brought from the Isle of Man and proposed a toast "to friendship." Nutkin and his cohorts were soon thoroughly drunk and totally unable to prevent the ensuing massacre.

Nutkin was the first to die as Rougina produced a

dagger from her tail and stabbed Nutkin to death. Unable to raise themselves from their drunken stupor Nutkin's "men" were soon dispatched the same way, none survived.

And, so born of blood, the Viking Republic of Formby was founded with Atta-Tac-Red as Supreme Leader. He and his descendants ruled with an iron fisted paw constantly at war with their cousins the Greys. Hemmed in on three sides with the sea at their backs, and living under the constant fear of invasion, this was the reality that was the Squirrel Republic of Formby.

THE COMMAND CENTRE

Right in the middle of Formby's pine tree woods set amidst the high canopy of the trees, was the command centre for the SRF (Squirrel Republic of Formby), camouflage netting making it virtually invisible to the naked eye.

All entrances to the intricate web of walkways were guarded by Red Squirrels; strikingly different from the soldiers on the beach, these all had black tails and black ear tufts, these were the Kemel Noir (The Blacks), the hereditary bodyguards of Kemel Red, all related by birth to the Supreme Leader of The Viking Republic of Formby, that same leader who now addressed his gathered commanders in his highly fortified war drey. Pointing at a map, he began, 'Anglesey has fallen to the Greys.'

There was a sharp intake of breath from the assembled commanders, Kemel Red continued.

'At first light we launched a Red Kite High

Altitude Milvus Bomber to overfly Anglesey, the pilots reported large numbers of our Red brothers dead on the beaches, and many more corpses floating in the sea. Comrades, Anglesey is lost to us but we have no time to grieve. The same returning surveillance flight overflew our eastern front and reported long columns of Greys transporting Pontoon bridges and scaling ladders. It is obvious to me that they will cross the Plains of Halsall under the cover of darkness to attack our drainage defence trenches at Wam Dyke Moss, should this attack succeed in crossing our trenches, it will be the end of us all. Gentlemen, we are outnumbered 500/1, but we have one thing the Greys don't have - "*air power.*"

> *The Viking Republic's ultimate weapon had been forged out of an unlikely alliance. Driven out of Anglesey by the nest-raiding Greys, the Red Kite population had sought refuge in the high pine trees of Formby.*

Initially wary of the Kites presence, a meeting was convened by Kemel Red with the leader of the Kites - Milvus Milverson, who, working on the principle that "my enemy's enemy is my friend," had agreed a mutual defence pact against the Greys.

Extensive training involving Red Squirrel Paratroops being carried on the backs of the Kites had proved incredibly successful, so successful that the Kites cousins, the Sparrow Hawk population of Formby, who shared the Kites hatred of the Greys had also joined the alliance. The Kites ability to hover at high altitude provided the Reds with the ultimate surveillance weapon, this coupled with the ability to carry large amounts of Pinecone Incendiary Bombs, made the Kites a fearsome weapon. The addition of the "**Screaming Death Sparrow Hawk Division**" had only enhanced this fearsome force.

A MEMBER OF THE SQUIRREL CORPS TAKES
QUICK WAY HOME

'So comrades, as the Greys seek to attack us using darkness as a shield, our friends the Kites will launch from a very high altitude a parachute flair that our special forces liberated from the humans old Lifeboat Station, this will illuminate the Grey forces where they are most vulnerable "The Plains of Halsall," and they will be exposed to the full force of our air power. The attack will be spear-headed by the Sparrow Hawk Screaming Death Division, all of which have been fitted with the latest air activated **Vuvuzela Dive Sirens** to strike fear into the enemy as well as the new lead wheel weight **Bridge Busting Bombs**.'

The lead wheel weights having been taken from the parked cars of the human visitors that poured into the Republic each weekend. In fact, so many wheel weights had been taken by Squirrel Special Forces that a new phenomenon had been born - "The Formby Wobble," this is what the human visitors called the mysterious vibrations that afflicted their cars after having visited Formby.

For months the Sparrow Hawks of Formby had resisted the offer to join the Kites in their alliance with the Reds, but a Grey nest-robbing incursion had made them realise that they had no choice but to join with the Kites and the Reds in the war against the Greys, and now too, they had become a highly effective unified fighting force.

'Comrades,' continued Kemel Red. 'The hour is upon us; I ask only one thing of you and that is you do your duty. Long live the Viking republic.'

RED KITE HIGH ALTITUDE MILVUS BOMBER
BEING READIED FOR COMBAT

THE FINAL SOLUTION

And so that night under the cover of darkness, as predicted by Kemel Red, a huge army of Grey Squirrels began to cross the Plains of Halsall, their initial advance only slowed by the large amount of bridge building timbers they carried. This apart, they made good progress and had reached the middle point of the crossing without incident.

This huge army was led by Adolphus Greyman, a highly decorated Commander, a veteran of numerous squirrel conflicts. He had promised the Lord High Squirrel of All England that he would initiate "**The Final Solution**"- the complete and utter destruction of the Red Squirrel population of Formby.

Suddenly night became day as the parachute flare erupted into the black night, exposing the Grey army to a merciless aerial bombardment as wave after wave of Sparrow Hawk Bombers strafed the forward columns of the

Grey forces, their Vuvuzela Sirens screaming. Such was the ferocity of the attack, that many Greys perished where they stood, others simply turned and ran, abandoning their equipment as they went.

The air attack had taken the Greys totally by surprise, all their equipment needed to cross the Red's defensive ditches lay smashed and broken.

As the last vestiges of the parachute flare spluttered and failed, returning the darkness to the land, an uneasy silence gripped the Plains of Halsall.

Now once again protected from attack by the darkness, Adolphus Greyman took reports from his shell-shocked commanders, they had lost almost all of their equipment, but most of the army remained intact, though widely scattered by the onslaught. The consensus from his assembled commanders was that they should retreat immediately under the cover of darkness before daybreak left them totally exposed to further air attacks. Greyman would have none of it, he'd been in difficult situations before and he was not going to lose his nerve now.

'Assemble all our forces we will launch a **Grey wave** on Wam Dyke Bridge.'

This news was greeted by the assembled commanders with deep trepidation and downright dismay, the prospect of a full-frontal *Grey wave* attack on Wam Dyke Bridge, the most heavily defended part of the Reds defences without scaling equipment, seemed utter madness.

> *Wam Dyke Bridge stood on an elevated section of the Leeds Liverpool Canal, well above the surrounding farmland, and could only be approached by a narrow roadway, meaning any attacking forces would be forced to funnel onto the roadway to attack the bridge.*

The Greys original battle plans had disregarded this option as "too costly in casualties and unlikely to succeed." Now Greyman addressed his commanders. 'The assault on the bridge will be the turning point in the war, we have come too far to lose - take this bridge and our forces will breakfast on a Formby Beach, free of the cursed Reds once and for all.'

THE BATTLE

The scene at the Red's headquarters could not be more different. The success of the air assault had exceeded their expectations, and though the battle had not yet been won, wild talk of regaining lost territories and old hunting grounds now filled the air. This sense of euphoria was soon brought crashing down by intelligence reports of large groups of Greys massing in the fields approaching Wam Dyke Bridge, these same reports indicated that an attack on the bridge was imminent.

Stripped of their airpower by the darkness their one and only parachute flare having been used, Commander Redman counselled his Officers.

'Gentlemen, the battle is not yet won, we must hold the bridge at all costs until daylight allows us to use our airpower once more - Wam Dyke must not fall.'

On the bridge the Red forces braced themselves for the assault that would now surely come, **Catapult Ballistas** bent and primed would unleash a barrage of pinecones filled with the same wheel weights that had made the aerial bombardment so effective. Out of site of the bridge's defenders a small group of Reds had managed to breech the canal bank in such a manner that they now had the power to unleash a "tidal wave" onto the Greys massing in the fields beneath them.

Unaware of the potential for disaster awaiting them the Grey army launched the "Grey Wave" attack on Wam Dyke Bridge, this tactic of using overwhelming numbers in a direct frontal assault had in the past secured the Greys many victories, but it had never been used against such a well defended position and was much more suited to open field warfare than the narrow roadway the Greys now poured onto.

Their presence on the roadway was met by a hail of pinecone incendiaries filled with hot lead that burned and seared. On and on the Grey wave poured, over the bodies of their fallen comrades, their sheer weight of numbers impelling them further forward towards the bridge.

The Reds situation was now becoming more and more desperate, they could delay no longer; the order was given, and the canal wall breached, unleashing a swirling torrent of water onto the roadway and surrounding fields. The effect was immediate, the Grey army was swept from the approaches to the bridge as if by a giant broom, they were helpless to resist, all the surrounding fields now turned to lakes full of drowning Greys their floating bodies giving witness to the folly of their attack on Wam Dyke Bridge.

THE RECKONING

As dawn finally broke over that momentous night, Adolphus Greyman surveyed the battlefield.

Now as the flood waters began to recede, the extent of the disaster was truly horrific. As far as the eye could see, Grey Squirrel corpses littered the landscape. Of the huge army that had left the Halsall Hills only a few stragglers remained.

Greyman had only saved himself by climbing up a telephone pole. From this elevated position he could see the Reds moving on the bridge, they appeared to be dragging Grey corpses nearer to the breach in the canal bank. Initially puzzled by this behaviour, it suddenly became clear to him that the Reds were making it look like the Greys were responsible for the damage to the canal bank. Once again, the Red's mastery of propaganda had prevailed.

The noise of an approaching vehicle sent the Reds running for cover. A team of canal workers sent to repair the leak, upon surveying the damage and the scattered Grey corpses, immediately concluded that Grey Squirrels tunnelling had caused the canal failure, and angry human voices could be heard.

'Stinking Grey vermin, we never have this trouble with the Reds.'

Whilst the workmen concerned themselves with repairing the damage to the canal, Greyman and a few followers slipped quietly away from the disaster.

VALIDATION

A Red Kite surveillance flight with a member of the **Squirrel Observer Corps** on board, overflew the battle scene at first light, and the news they brought back to the Red headquarters provoked wild celebration amongst the assembled commanders.

Finally, Kemel Red managed to regain control over his jubilant commanders.

'Comrades today we have inflicted the greatest defeat imaginable on our most implacable foe, they sought to end our way of life and indeed to eradicate the Red Squirrel entirely.'

'The magnitude of our victory will live long in our history only if we survive to tell it. So as from today, the age of conscription into the defence forces of our Republic will be lowered to three months old, male and female there will be no exceptions. The refugees from Anglesey after medical checks, will begin training with our forces and in time will form the *Innis Môn Battalion* which will be fully integrated into our defence forces. Any found to be medically unfit, will be re-united with their rafts and cast out to sea. The price of our freedom must be eternal vigilance and total dedication to the preservation of our Viking Republic.'

FACING HIS MAKER

Having made the long journey back to his base in the Halsall Hills, Adolphus Greyman was not expecting a hero's welcome, but as he stood in chains before the Lord High Squirrel, he feared the worst.

Sat upon a raised throne, the Lord High Squirrel cast an intimidating figure, resplendent in the regalia of his office, his grey fur tinged with the white of age he looked up from the papers before him.

'You Sir, left here with the largest Grey Squirrel army that this country has ever seen, promising to rid me of the Reds once and for all, and where is that army now?' Greyman attempted to answer but was cut short.

'I'll tell you where it is, the dead bodies of our finest troops are being collected from the Plains of Halsall by the humans and then burnt in large bonfires lest their dead bodies should contaminate their beloved Red Squirrel population.'

'You sir have failed in your duty, you have lost an army, and more importantly you have lost the propaganda war. The humans persecute us with a vengeance, convinced that we were responsible for the failure of the canal and the flooding that did so much damage to their crops. We cannot venture out into the countryside for fear of being shot by vengeful farmers, and all the while the Reds are safe in their human-made Squirrel Reserve performing tricks for the gullible visitors who flock to see them. This campaign has been a total disaster and you Sir, must pay the ultimate price "**Mu-tailation.**"

The very word chilled Adolphus Greyman to the bone.

'Please my Lord give me a soldier's death, anything would be better than the shame and ignominy of being a squirrel without a tail. Without a tail I am nothing, cast into exile, no Drey would be open to me, no paw would be extended to me I would be shunned by all, please my Lord I beg you have mercy.'

The Lord High Squirrel was not moved by Greyman's pleas.

'You will be taken from here to the *Place of Sorrows* where the sentence of mu-tailation will be carried out. After your tail has been cut from your living body it will be burnt on a bonfire so that all will see what awaits those who fail me. **'TAKE HIM AWAY.'**

GUILLOTINE MU-TAILATION

And so, as the once mighty Adolphus Grey-man was dragged away to meet his fate and with the Greys unable to venture forth in daylight hours for fear of being shot, an uneasy peace descended on this little part of Lancashire.

WAM DYKE CONFERENCE

Kemel Red, never a one to rest on his laurels, convened a meeting of his Total Security Council. This took place in the "Drey of the Leader," a long abandoned former Lifeboat Station now totally engulfed by the giant sand dunes that roamed the Formby shore, its whereabouts and exact location long lost to all. It had been rediscovered by pure chance, after a savage storm had scoured the dunes uncovering a drainage pipe.

Squirrel Special Forces on anti-invasion exercises had decided to explore it and were amazed to find that the pipe ran directly into the lost Lifeboat Station. When news of this discovery was conveyed to Kemel Red he immediately imposed a total news blackout, any talk of the discovery or its whereabouts was to risk mu-tailation and certain death.

Using Red Squirrel dissidents taken from the Re-education Camps and Nicotine Mines that were a feature of Kemel Red's regime, the building's interior was cleared of sand, the former Lifeboat hall was converted into a conference room, with a Command Bunker for the Great Leader and his family.

With a constant flow of water diverted from the nearby golf course at hand, and large amounts of stored pinecones as food, the Drey of the Leader provided the perfect place for the Wam Dyke Victory Conference which Vermillion Red the half-sister of the Great Leader now addressed.

Speaking from a raised platform she looked down on the assembled "family."

'I will open this Conference with a pledge of undying loyalty to Kemel Red our Great Leader, he is the heartbeat of our Republic and the military genius who gave us the greatest victory in our history.'

And suddenly there he was as if by magic, the Great Leader appeared on stage.

His appearance was immediately greeted by every member of the extended family jumping to their feet and clapping their paws wildly. This continued for quite some time, each one fearful to be seen to be less enthusiastic than the other, lest this showed disloyalty to the Great Leader.

Just as it seemed that the clapping could be sustained no longer, Vermillion Red raised her paw and signalled them to stop. Taking this cue, Kemel

Red strode centre stage, resplendent in his Field Marshal's uniform and wearing around his neck the Great Seal of Office surmounted with Pine-cone Clusters, standing there without speaking until a single voice from the floor shouted

'Lead us great leader, where you lead we will follow.'

Chants of' lead us, leads us, lead us,' rang though all those assembled. Vermillion Red's body language could not hide the immense satisfaction she felt as she purred and preened in her stage-management of the event, out of earshot of everyone other than the Great Leader she whispered... *'now...'*

Kemel Red raised both paws in the air, the room fell instantly silent.

'The time of defence is over. Our great victory at Wam Dyke has brought the Grey Army in the North to its knees, we cannot let them regroup, we must attack them before they are strong enough to threaten us once more. I can reveal to you today that our *Chemical Weapons Team*, brilliantly led by Professor Torben Red, have developed a weapon that will end the numerical superiority of the Greys once and for all.'

Wild cheering ensued, quickly brought to an end by the raised paw of Kemel Red.

'This weapon will allow us not only to regain full control of all of Lancashire and Merseyside but also to regain Anglesey'

More wild cheering.........

Kemel red continued.

'I now call upon Professor Torben Red to address you, I need not tell you that as members of the Total Security Committee you are bound by a blood oath of secrecy.'

With this Torben Red strode on to the stage, a tall figure by squirrel standards his shock white hair matching his laboratory coat.

'PCP is a synthetic substance we have engineered from palm oil discarded on to our beaches by passing ships. When mixed with nicotine waste, also dumped on our beaches by the meddling humans and with the addition of *Ingredient X*, it produces a highly addictive substance, that when ingested or even inhaled, causes total loss of cerebral cognitive function, in short, it drives the Greys mad.'

More wild cheering followed Torben Red as he left the stage paw in paw with the Great Leader.

After countless pledges of loyalty from the assembled gathering, the Conference was finally brought to an end.

AFTERGLOW

Later while he relaxed in his private quarters, drinking Pinenip Brandy with Vermillion Red, and as they basked in the glow of self-satisfied mutual admiration; a message was brought to them by Kemel Red's Adjutant and half-brother Betterred, bringing the news that a half starved Grey Squirrel, minus his tail and carrying a white flag had been detained by Wam Dyke border guards.

On interrogation he claimed to be Adolphus Greyman, former Commander of the Grey Army of the North, and that he had information that he was prepared to exchange for food and sanctuary:

"Kill him, we have no need of traitors, cut off his head to match his tail' answered Kemel Red.

However Vermillion Red was more cautious

'My brother you are right as always, but should we not listen to what he has to say? If it is of no value, rather than a quick death, give him a painful lingering death in the Nicotine Mines.'

Quick to temper to the point of rashness, but

valuing his sister's opinion, he had Adolphus Grey-man brought before him.

Bound in fencing wire liberated from the humans, now deprived of his tail and clearly starving, he bore no resemblance to the once great Commander who had secretly met with Kemel Red in the months before the Wam Dyke Battle. At these meetings Greyman had demanded the immediate surrender of the Formby Colony, he even offered safe passage to Scotland to Kemel Red and his family.

Kemel Red had initially seemed receptive to this offer, though all the while secretly developing his *Air Weapons Program* with the Kites.

Finally, after numerous meetings and delays Greyman was convinced that Kemel Red would never give up his control of the Republic, and so he launched the invasion, with all its subsequent catastrophic consequences.

'Come to offer me free passage to Scotland have you?' said Kemel Red unable to stop himself from gloating over Greyman's now wretched state. 'Why should I show mercy to you?' continued Kemel Red, 'you that promised that pompous old fool who calls himself "The Lord High Squirrel," that you would solve the Formby Red Squirrel "*problem*" once and for all. Speak now for your very presence offends me.'

Greyman replied, trying to gather the last of his

dignity by standing tall... not easy when bound limb and paw with fencing wire.

'You may have won the battle, but you will never win the war as long as the Lord High Squirrel draws breath. Not all Greys agree with his war-mongering, the huge loss of life at Wam Dyke has caused many to question his leadership. Remove him and the Grey Peace Faction would call for an end to the war, think of your legacy "Kemel Red the Great leader" who ended fifty years of war.

Vermillion Red was first to reply mockingly, her voice purring with menace.

'And how would we remove him from power, ask him to leave?'

'No, you would have to kill him, said Greyman, and to do that you would first have to get into Holborn Hill.'

HOLBORN HILL

Holborn Hill, the most secure Grey Squirrel Fortress in all of Britain, thought to be impregnable, was in an abandoned Stone Quarry. Set on the side of a hill, it dominated all the surrounding countryside as far as the coastal forests of Formby. It was the Headquarters of the Grey Army of the North, and also the residence of the Lord High Squirrel.

Cosmo Marmajuke Grey had inherited the title of Lord High Squirrel from his father Manyshades Grey, who had created the title for himself after successfully leading a campaign, that, from its base in Northumbria, had ravaged the length and breadth of Britain, driving all before them, forcing the Red Squirrel population to the verge of extinction. The one thorn in his side had been Formby. Numerous campaigns against the "Viking Republic" had all failed, even as he approached death it still obsessed him.

Clutching Cosmo to him and struggling for breath his last words were, 'promise me my son, you will avenge me, rid me of that accursed Formby once and for all.'

Manyshades death had come quickly and had been totally unexpected, leading to dark rumours of poisoning being levelled at the Reds.

All of this fuelled Cosmo in his thirst to destroy The Formby Colony, and this had propelled him into the disastrous decision to launch the invasion that would fail so catastrophically at the Battle of Wam Dyke.

Now as he sat and brooded in his Holborn Hill Citadel only one thing was on his mind.... Formby!

The loss of life at Wam Dyke had been so great that it now threatened his ability to provide troops to garrison Anglesey. His provisional Governor on the island had reported capturing Red Mercenaries from the Isle Of Man, fanatical fighters, ideologically driven by an intense hatred of the Greys they had banded together with remnants of the Red Army of Anglesey and were now threatening to overrun Anglesey.

The situation was now so bad that the Governor of Anglesey had asked for permission to retreat to the Welsh mainland.

The response to this request was swift and brutal. Anglesey was to be held at all costs, any Squirrel failing to do his duty would suffer mu-tailation and his family would suffer the same fate.

Despite all this, Cosmo's obsession with Formby would not leave him.

WEAPONS OF MASS DESTRUCTION

It is said that nature abhors a vacuum and that the status quo can only hold if things remain the same, but after the Battle of Wam Dyke Bridge everything changed. The Grey Squirrels, once so dominant the length and breadth of Britain, now beleaguered in their fortresses like some latter-day crusaders, looked out upon the land that they once ruled but now feared to tread.

Their Leader the Lord High Squirrel of All Britain and the Isles, Cosmo Marmajuke Grey, walked the battlements of his Holborn Hill Fortress, his demeanour soured by intelligence reports that his former Commander of the Grey Army of the North, Adolphus Greyman, had sought sanctuary in the Red Squirrel Republic of Formby.

Greyman was in command at the fateful battle of Wam Dyke Bridge and was held to be culpable for the ensuing disastrous defeat and loss of life. At his Court Martial he was found guilty of "high crimes and misdemeanours," and sentenced to death, but Cosmo, incandescent with rage refused to accept the verdict, instead, insisting such was the magnitude of his crimes that only one sentence was possible.... Mu-tailation. The severing of a Squirrel's tail from its living body by means of a guillotine and the tail's destruction on a bonfire, was an ancient punishment that had been mostly consigned to the history books and had not been used for decades.

The punishment duly carried out, Greyman was cast out from the safety of the fortress and left to forage in an increasingly dangerous countryside, hiding by day and travelling by night, constantly on his guard for bands of marauding Pine Martens, who, emboldened by the Greys defeat at Wam Dyke had taken to hunting them down for food. Pine Martens regarded Grey Squirrels as a delicacy. Kebabbed and barbequed were the most popular ways of serving this delicacy and they had been off the menu for many years, due to the Greys being able to garrison the countryside and protect their own from rapacious Pine Marten predation. But now, stripped of the garrisons that once protected them, the Greys had now become the hunted where once they had been the hunter.

BBQ GREY SQUIRREL A PINE MARTEN DELICACY

CABIN HILL

Hubris is only Hubris if you let it get to you. Adolphus Greyman's fall from grace had been spectacular and would have laid lesser beings low, but not Greyman. After seeking sanctuary in the Formby Republic, he had initially been forced to work in the Nicotine Mines, while the Great Leader of the Squirrel Republic, Kemel Red, decided what to do with him and the intelligence that he brought.

The work in the mines was ferociously hard, and normally reserved for any in the Republic who had the temerity to question the supremacy of the Great Leader and his family, and as such, was regularly supplied with new labour as neighbour spied on neighbour in evermore desperate attempts to prove their loyalty to the regime.

Average life expectancy in the Nicotine Mines was a month for the able bodied, but for a Grey Squirrel without a tale and subjected to constant physical and verbal abuse about his colour and lack of balance from his fellow inmates, that expectancy would have been much shorter had fate not intervened once more.

The nicotine waste dumped on the Formby sand dunes for over fifty years by the humans, had once been well inland of the Irish Sea, but time and tide were beginning to collapse the giant dunes that over the years had carpeted the waste and hidden it from view. Now, due to the hungry sea constantly tearing into the dunes, large amounts of nicotine were found dumped on the beach by the outgoing tide, making mining for nicotine no longer necessary as it could be collected under cover of darkness from the seashore and transported to the "chemical weapons facility" at nearby Cabin Hill.

Cabin Hill was the reason for the Nicotine mining, the very name being an oxymoron. Once the highest sand dune on the Formby coast, and formerly used as a navigation aid for ships entering the Port of Liverpool, it was now reduced to a hole in the ground by human "sand-winning". This being a metaphor for the destruction of the environment for financial gain, the removed sand being sold to the construction industry. Now a desolate godforsaken place, abutting a military live firing range, and not troubled by human visitors, even the National Trust's, notorious busybodies stayed clear, saying they were letting the area "revert back to nature." Cabin Hill's only residents had been Newts and Natterjack toads until the Red Squirrels moved in and built a "chemical weapons facility".

Here, under the watchful eye of Torben Red Chief Scientist and Minister for War, the deadly *chemical weapon "**Nuttachoc**"* was being manufactured. Formally known as PCP (Pine Cone Psychosis), the name having been changed by Kemel Red who decided PCP lacked oomph!!

Nuttachoc had been created by blending nicotine waste and palm oil with a third "unknown" classified ingredient. The palm oil had been dumped into the sea by passing ships and recovered from the beach. The Nuttachoc programme was the Red Squirrel "game-changer." This was the *wonder weapon* that would address the numerical supremacy that the Greys had over the Reds once and for all, but its development had come at great cost. Hundreds had perished, thousands were on the brink of starvation, but still the work progressed.

The use of nicotine waste as a constituent part of the weapon had come about when a large rabbit warren built into the side of a dune, was extended into the nicotine dump. Almost immediately rabbits became ill and started dying at an alarming rate. This fact was not lost upon Torben Red who had been searching for years for substances that could be used in his chemical weapons program.

Nicotine mining began after laboratory experiments had produced the deadly toxin Nuttachoc. The effects of Nuttachoc poisoning were instantaneous and nearly always fatal. *The production of Nuttachoc was equally as lethal as the poison itself.*

A leak from the plant resulted in an epidemic of what would become known as Squirrel Pox which swept through the colony causing many deaths. The name "Squirrel Pox" having been devised by Gurballs Red the Propaganda Minister, who, addressing the large crowds of fearful Reds gathered outside his "Ministry of Constant Truth," claimed that the Grey Squirrels under the leadership of the "Demented Megalomaniac Son of Satan, Cosmo Marmajuke Grey," had been responsible for introducing the so called pox into the colony, thus covering up the real source of the deaths and driving the colonies xenophobia to new heights.

His master stroke had been in the transportation of the bodies of the victims of the leak at Cabin Hill to the Squirrel Reserve at Formby, where they were placed next to the body of a dead Grey Squirrel; a prisoner who had died in the same leak. Years of Red Squirrel propaganda would do the rest. All that time performing tricks, running up trees, posing for selfies had not been in vain.

True to form, the gullible woolly headed humans, in the form of the National Trust, bought it hook line and sinker, proclaiming that the Grey Squirrels had carried a virus which had infected their beloved Reds, and henceforth they would be redoubling their efforts to eradicate the Greys from Formby for ever.

OUT OF THE DEPTHS OF DESPAIR

Adolphus Greyman, his back bent double by the weight of the nicotine basket on his back, climbed the rickety ladder towards the light far above him. Ladder after ladder until he finally emerged blinking into the light of the mine entrance.

For two weeks he had endured the conditions of the mine. His fellow prisoners, all Reds, were deeply hostile to his colour and presence and lost no opportunity to make his life even more wretched than it was, spitting on his nuts, ridiculing his lack of tail and subsequent lack of balance and deriding him even further by constantly jeering and calling him *wobbly* whenever he came into their presence.

Greyman's famed resilience along with his body was on the point of collapse. The thought of another forced march through the giant dunes at night to the Cabin Hill Plant, filled him with dread. Standing with his nicotine basket at his feet he awaited his turn to be "*manacled*," (all prisoners on the march were manacled together to prevent any attempt at escape). This procedure was carried out by the Revernant's, squirrels who had been sent to the mines because they had been born as the result of interracial acts of procreation between the Reds and Greys. The parents of such progeny if found, would be immediately executed and the offspring sent to the mines to be trained as guards.

Deprived of normal family life and emotional contact, these orphans subsequently ran the mines with a rod of iron, no cruelness was beyond them. So, when two of the Revernants instead of manacling Greyman, pulled him out of the line of prisoners and dragged him to the shower block, he feared the worst. The Revernants used the shower block to administer punishment beatings, which often proved fatal to the unfortunate recipient.

Instead of the expected violence, Greyman was provided with Pinecone soap and allowed to use the guards shower. After showering, (the tin can shower being strangely effective) and with the smell of the pine soap still in his nostrils, came the ultimate shock….. On the wall was a car hub cap which doubled as a mirror. For the first time in months, and now cleansed of the detritus of the mine, Greyman caught sight of his own reflection and he was stunned by what he saw. All that contact with nicotine waste had coloured his once grey coat and now from the tips of his ears to the stump of his tail he was **BRIGHT RED!!**

BETTER RED
THAN DEAD!

Vermillion Red, the half-sister of Kemel Red the Supreme Leader of the Squirrel Republic of Formby, paced her private quarters anxiously. Long regarded as the "Eminence Rouge" and the real power within the Republic, she had been party to the decision to release Adolphus Grey-man from the mines, seeing him as a source of intelligence that should be exploited, and that his connections with the Grey Squirrel "Peace Move-ment" should be explored further, rather than consigning him to a certain death working in the Nicotine Mines.

This decision carried great risk to herself, as it went directly against Kemel Red's orders that Greyman should be 'left in the mines to rot.' As more time elapsed and still no sign of Greyman she became more and more agitated, her mood not lifted by the arrival of Betterred the Supreme Leader's Chief of Staff and half-brother, and also Vermillion Red's cousin.

He was greeted by Vermillion Red screaming at him.

'Where is he, something must have gone wrong he should have been here by now.'

'Calm yourself sister,' intoned Betterred.

The pejorative use of the word **sister** enraging Vermillion Red even further. Squirrel relationships were extremely complex and hierarchical and though he was her cousin, he could indeed have been her brother and therefore a full brother to the Great Leader and as such his likely successor, but by this Byzantine metric, Vermillion Red would have an equal claim to be the next in line.

The Great Leader had fathered countless offspring by numerous partners, but none of them had shown themselves fit to inherit the leadership of the Republic. Overindulged and overfed, these pampered progenies both male and female strode the Republic, their sole purpose other than the pursuit of pleasure, seemed to be scheming and plotting amongst themselves as to who would inherit the leadership of the Republic

Kemel Red would not countenance any talk of his succession.

The military success at the battle of Wam Dyke had totally gone to his head, deluding himself to such an extent, that he now declared himself the reincarnation on earth of the Republic's Founder and God-like figure Attatack Red, and as such would live for ever, making any talk of succession unnecessary.

This dangerous nonsense had forced Vermillion

Red and Betterred into an uneasy alliance, it was their joint decision to free Greyman. Any further discourse as to Greyman's whereabouts rendered useless by a completely cloaked and hooded figure being dragged into the room by two of Betterred's bodyguards.

'Uncover him we have waited long enough' demanded Vermillion Red.

'Madam I must warn you he has changed since you saw him last,' answered one of the bodyguards

'I care not for his wellbeing or appearance, uncover him,' replied Vermillion Red.

With that, the hood and the cloak were removed from Greyman's body. Betterred was the first to react, Vermillion Red seemed stunned into silence.

'What trickery is this? I ordered you to bring Greyman to me, not some down and out Red without a tail, you will pay dearly for this treachery.'

'My Lord Bettered it is I, do you not recognise me?'

Betterred could not believe his ears, the instantly recognisable voice of Adolphus Greyman one-time leader of the Grey Squirrel Army of the North, was now issuing forth from what appeared to be a dilapidated Red Squirrel. The voice continued.

'Do not be frightened by my colour, the nicotine waste has made me just like you, I can assure you that it offends me equally, but is not our enterprise greater than the colour of my coat?'

TIME AND A TIDE
TO SQUIRREL AFFAIRS

In Holborn Hill there is much excitement, a messenger has arrived from Anglesey, and for the first time in many months it brings good news.

The Red Alliance that had almost driven the Greys off the Island had been stopped in their tracks. Unlike Red Squirrels, Greys cared not for bloodlines and racial purity but only for ability; so, when Anglesey teetered on the brink of disaster, the Governor was replaced along with the whole officer corps by cadets straight out of the Holborn Hill military academy calling themselves the "Grey Wolves," who, realising the gravity of the situation, had taken the highly dangerous decision to cross to Anglesey by sea. Unable to use the heavily guarded beaches of Formby, they had set off from nearby Southport taking advantage of an exceptionally high tide that allowed the cadets to launch their craft by means of "The Bog Hole Channel," a long silted up waterway, only useable at certain times of the year when the high tide would force water into the channel at such a rate it became a torrent pouring in, and equally pouring out when the tide turned. The timing of the launch had to be at the very moment that the tide went out.

For all their claimed differences, the craft launched by the cadets into the outrushing Bog Hole Channel greatly resembled the rafts used by the Red refugees fleeing Anglesey, namely, plastic bottles tied together with string, and one by one these little craft shot out to sea, propelled out over the sandbanks by the fast receding tidal tow and into the Irish Sea and on to Anglesey.

The Grey cadets arrival in Anglesey had been welcomed with great enthusiasm by the besieged Grey garrison and coincided with a ferocious bout of infighting amongst their Red enemies. Fighting under the banner of the "Red Army of Anglesey" this disparate force had only one thing in common, a visceral hatred of Greys, and now in the moment of their greatest triumph they chose to throw all the hard-won gains away by fighting each other. The reason for this conflict, as in most disputes was *Politics*!

The Red Army contained two distinct factions, the Ynys Mon indigenous Welsh speaking Squirrels, and the Ellan Vannin, mercenaries from the Isle of Man who had little or no grasp of the Welsh language. So when the Ynys Mon decided that after defeating the Greys, they would make it compulsory for all Squirrels to speak nothing but Welsh, and making this a condition of any subsequent citizenship, this incensed the Ellan Vannin to such a degree that they threatened to leave the *alliance* and return to The Isle of Man.

Angry words soon changed to angry deeds, pitching former allies against each other with evermore disastrous consequences, culminating in all out warfare while the bemused Greys looked on hardly able to believe their luck at this turn of events.

IF YOU DON'T
USE IT
YOU LOSE IT.

Kemel Red didn't do visits, spending most of his time in his bunker deep beneath the "Great Drey of the People," living with a constant fear of assassination and

even his recent determination that he was now a "God"

and immortal had left him with nagging doubts!

Now with his God delusion fuelling his paranoia to new heights he began to see conspiracy everywhere.

Security in Kemel Red's Republic was controlled by BOSS (Bureau of Squirrel Security), its director, Redfist Red, also his half-brother, reported directly to the Great Leader in person.

At his daily briefing Redfist Red had to tell the Great Leader that his agents had discovered Adolphus Greyman had been released from the mines on the orders of Vermillion Red and that his Adjutant and half-brother Betterred had been complicit in the release

Kemel Red was apoplectic with rage, how dare anyone, even someone as close to him as Vermillion Red go behind his back.

Ranting and raving, and at times foaming from the mouth, he spewed vitriol in all directions, claiming that the Republic did not deserve his "divine presence".

On and on he ranted, until sheer exhaustion forced him to flop back onto his elevated throne totally spent by his exertions.

Redfist Red had seen it all before and duly waited for the storm to cease. When it appeared that Kemel Red had regained control of his emotions, Redfist Red told him that his agent, one of Betterred's bodyguards had overheard Vermillion Red discussing with the newly liberated Adolphus Greyman, the possibility of entering into peace negotiations with a moderate Grey Squirrel faction, who sought an end to the war.

'End to the war I'll give them an end to the World, those snivelling ingrates don't deserve my genius, they will rue the day that they tried to defy my will. Get me Torben Red now,' screamed Kemel Red.

As a scientist Torben Red was unequalled. His work on the Nuttachoc program had given him great power and prestige. This power had been given to him by Kemel Red who could just as easily take it away from him and this was acknowledged by the speed that Torben Red rushed to his master's side when summoned.

Entering the bunker, after numerous body searches, Torben Red was met by the sight of Kemel Red pacing up and down and clearly highly agitated. He acknowledged Torben Red telling him.

'I want you to plan an assault on Holborn hill using Nuttachoc.'

KEMEL RED

ON A RARE EXCURSION OUTSIDE HIS BUNKER

THE TROUBLE
WITH
DEMOCRACY

Cosmo Marmajuke Grey heartened by the news from Anglesey, decided that the situation there was no longer critical, thus allowing him to turn his attention back to Formby.

The tremendous losses sustained by the war had weakened his control of the Grey Squirrel Population, and voices of discontent once muted were now strident in condemnation of his handling of the war. "The Knutte," the Parliament that was normally no more than a supine talking shop egged on by the Speaker, suddenly decided to assert itself by calling for Cosmo to abandon the war with the Formby Republic and to enter into peace talks immediately.

The "Speaker of the House," Wocreb Grey, was unusual in that he wasn't even a Squirrel, but an orphaned Weasel that had been adopted by a Squirrel family and he had only been promoted to his current position in the name of diversity.

Cosmo argued that by calling off the war before

peace talks had even started, would weaken his hand in any subsequent negotiations, and that the best way to get a good deal was to continue the war.

When this approach was roundly defeated by the Parliament, aided and abetted by Wocreb, Cosmo did what all good dictators do, he "Prologged" the Parliament, in effect shutting it down.

This was greeted by loud howls of dismay and much singing of protest songs.

"Prologging" was an ancient power harking back to the days when the Greys were ruled by a hereditary monarchy. The monarchy was side-lined when Cosmos' father, Manyshades Grey had seized power, but the largely symbolic monarchy had retained the power of "Prologgation."

Its present incumbents, Queen Doddery and her consort Prince Fillup, aided and abetted by their gormless son Farles Duke of Noware and his equally ghastly wife Pamilla Countess of Nothing, would assent to anything Cosmo put in front of them, in exchange for "Conenip" brandy and some Cashew nuts.

**AT HOME WITH QUEEN DODDERY AND
HER CONSORT PRINCE FILLUP**

So, Parliament despite endless renditions of 'we shall overcome' and howls of anguish, was duly "Prologged." The actual process of "Prologging" involved "*The Log,*" this was the Seat of the Speaker being removed from the Parliament by throwing it out of an upstairs window!!

> *Wocreb rather unwisely had tied himself to the Log in an attempt to prevent its removal. This failed spectacularly when the soldiers sent by Cosmo, simply picked up the log with Wocreb still attached, and threw it out of the window!!*

Now that democracy had been dealt with, Cosmo got back to the business of running the war.

THE GREAT
LEADER
KNOWS BEST

Kemel Red had no such difficulties with any sort of Parliament, or restraint, he knew what was best for his kind and if they didn't like it he would have them killed. This philosophy had served all previous members of his dynasty very well and Kemel Red saw no reason to change. In fact, his recent self-elevation to a God, had only strengthened his feeling of infallibility.

Summoning Torben Red to his side, and despite hearing his misgivings about using Nuttachoc to assault the Holborn Hill Citadel, he would countenance no talk of delay, even Gurballs Red the Propaganda Minister, who had been hurriedly summoned by Torben Red to join with him and the Great Leader in his Bunker, offered a note of caution, such use of "chemical weapons" and the large amount of attendant casualties, coupled with possible pollution of the water courses, would risk the intrusion of the humans into their affairs, with all the dangers that this would bring to their cause.

Kemel Red would have none of it.

'What is the use of "*wonder weapons*" if you don't use them?'

Turning to Torben Red…. 'as Minister for War, I demand that you launch operation **Golgotha** immediately.'

WHAT TO DO
ABOUT
THE WAR

Kemel Red was not the only one to have spies, so when Vermillion Red was informed of the Great Leader's plan to launch operation "**Golgotha**" (The Place of Skulls), she was horrified. She knew only too well the efficacy of Nuttachoc, having witnessed the carnage caused by the so called "Squirrel Pox" incident, and this had been her motivation in freeing Adolphus Greyman so that the possibility of some kind of peace deal could be explored, to put an end to the madness before it put an end to them all.

Her initial talks with Greyman had been disappointing to say the very least. It turned out that The Grey Peace Movement that Greyman represented, had been led by Weasel Wocreb and since his unfortunate death, it had been taken over by Farles Duke of Noware the heir apparent to the Grey Squirrel Throne, who saw it as an opportunity to remove Cosmo and reinstall the Monarchy.

Vermillion Red's Agents had presented her with a less than flattering portrayal of his character, saying that he was a notorious dullard, with a penchant for talking to trees, seldom sober and addicted to his beliefs that he was born to rule. Highly unpopular even with his own people, he would be regarded as the very last person able to form a coalition that could bring an end to the war.

Vermillion Red had badly miscalculated Greyman's worth. The risk she and Betterred had taken in freeing him now imperilled their lives. It would only be a matter of time before Kemel Red found out. Something had to be done, and fast.

Rushing to the Great Leader's Bunker she was initially denied entrance by the "*Kemel Noir*," (Kemel Red's hereditary bodyguards). Vermillion Red now feared the worst as she was forced to endure the indignity of a full body search before being shown into the Bunker. She was dismayed to see that the Great Leader was not alone, but deep in conversation with Torben Red, Minister for War and Gurballs Red the Propaganda Minister, and they appeared to be looking at a map, the conversation ceasing on her entrance, as an icy silence gripped the room.

Finally, Kemel Red acknowledged his long-time confidante without looking up from the map.

'As I am sure that you know by now, I have ordered Operation Golgotha to be implemented. We are just finalising the details, shall I tell you the details so that you may impart them to your Grey friend, oh I forgot he's Red now!!'

The look on Gurballs Red's face was of pure pleasure, he had bitterly resented Vermillion Red's closeness to the Great Leader and could not contain his pleasure at her situation. Gurballs Red had been born with an underdeveloped paw which gave him a rather unfortunate way of moving, in fact he slithered, and in an unguarded moment Vermillion Red had referred to him as "*the Snake*."

From this remark the seeds of a great enmity had been sown, only Vermillion Reds' closeness to the Great leader had saved her from the inevitable "fatal accident" that befell anyone who dared ridicule his deformity.

Vermillion Red had an instance to save her life, and she seized it with both her paws

Throwing herself at the Great Leaders feet, she pleaded with him that the release of Greyman and her apparent treachery had all been part of her plan to persuade the Grey Leadership to enter into peace talks, which would involve Greyman returning to Holborn Hill as a "Peace Envoy," where he would meet with The Lord High Squirrel and his Commanders. At this meeting Greyman would tell them that he brought an offer of peace and reconciliation.

Gurballs Red had heard enough:

'This is rubbish, you have conspired against our Great Leader and now you try to save yourself with this embarrassment of lies, what possible outcome could any such meeting produce that would justify your treachery?'

Grasping the moment, Vermillion Red standing up as tall as she could her tail now ramrod straight, and in a voice that portrayed none of her inner turmoil, replied:

'The death of the Lord High Sheriff Cosmo Fry and all of his Generals.'

Finally, Kemel Red spoke.

'Just how would these deaths be achieved?'

Vermillion Red realising that she had Kemel Red's interest and playing the family card continued,

'By use of a device, my brother.'

Gurballs Red, could not let this play out any longer.

'No one could get into such a meeting carrying a bomb, they would be searched from ear to tale, inside and out, before meeting with Cosmo Fry. His security precautions are legendary, how could you possibly conceal such a device?'

Vermillion Red's speed of thought was legendary and now that all eyes were upon her, she did not disappoint.

'The device would not be a bomb; it would be far more effective than that! **The device would be Adolphus Greyman**!'

'And he would do this?' said an incredulous Kemel Red.

'He would do it my brother, because he wouldn't know he was doing it.'

Continuing, Vermillion Red outlined her plan to send Greyman as a "Peace Envoy," and he had agreed, providing that he was fitted with a prosthetic tale, and that we treated his coat so that it regained its natural Grey colour.

'And that's where I come in' said the previously silent Torben Red, who had watched the drama unfolding in front of him with mixed emotions.

No fan of Vermillion Red but fearing she would be replaced by Gurballs Red and the threat to his position that would bring; he threw Vermillion Red a lifeline:

'Some time ago Vermillion Red came to Cabin Hill to explore with me the possibility of making Nuttachoc into a liquid, and if so, how could it's instantly lethal effect be retarded or masked, so that someone unknowingly treated with this liquid would live long enough to perform whatever mission he had been tasked with, before succumbing to the inevitable consequences, while also consigning everyone he came in contact with to the same certain death.'

Suddenly Kemel Red shouted excitedly, 'and you would use the turncoat Greyman. Using him to destroy his own kind! **Brilliant!!!** You are indeed my sister. How could I have ever doubted you?'

IGNORANCE
IS BLISS

Cosmo having dealt with Parliament, returned to the business of prosecuting the war with a new found relish.

Such was his good humour that he was even prepared to give Farles Duke of Noware an audience. Normally he would have just said that matters of State were not conducive to such a meeting, and declined, but emboldened by his dealings with Parliament, he agreed to the audience but with one proviso... that being... that Farles came without his constant companion Pamilla Duchess of Nothing.

Before Pamilla married Farles she had been promised to Cosmo by way of arranged marriage. Pamilla being of "Royal Blood" would give the Manyshades Grey *Dynasty* the legitimacy it so craved, but at the very last moment she had eloped with her cousin Farles, leaving the young Cosmo distraught.

Cosmo was not a forgiving man and would miss no opportunity to remind Pamilla who was the real power in the land.

Sitting in the anti-chamber while Farles was

summoned into Cosmo's presence, Pamilla was left to reflect that maybe she had "backed the wrong horse" all those years ago.

Cosmo thought Farles a pompous fool and had many times thought of abolishing the Monarchy entirely, but it had proved itself a useful tool in his battle with Parliament, so he had decided to give it a "little more rope!"

'My Lord High Squirrel I bring you greetings and felicitations from Her Majesty, I trust we find you well,' intoned Farles in a voice so affected it made Cosmo wince.

'Tolerably well' in a voice loaded with sarcasm he replied adding, 'and why has Your Highness done me the great honour of visiting my humble home?'

In truth there was nothing about the Lord High Squirrel's home that was humble. Hewn from the rock by human miners and long abandoned by them, it had been repurposed into private quarters that Farles would have died to possess, especially given his own impoverished situation. So well insulated from the cold by Pinestraw wall hangings, and with every floor covered in the same way, it really was ridiculously warm even in the depths of winter, and as it was now the height of summer, hotter than ever.

Cosmo as usual was oblivious to the heat. (Historians would later claim that Cosmo suffered from *temperature dysmorphia*, an inability to regulate his own body temperature, resulting in the fact that he constantly felt cold).

Farles however was now feeling far from cold!

The sauna like temperature in Cosmo's quarters was causing him to sweat profusely, dark stains now streaked his fur and perspiration dripped from the end of his nose causing Cosmo much amusement.

'I have a matter of great importance to lay before you Lord High Squirrel, I have received peace overtures from the Formby Republic that I think you should consider very seriously, I believe them to be genuine and sincere and I would ask you to consider them in the same manner.'

Cosmo bristled,

'Your Highness should be very careful about meddling in Affairs of State however well intentioned, some would think communicating with an enemy at a time of war could be construed as treason and should be dealt with in the prescribed manner Mu-tailation.'

At the mention of the word "Mu-tailation," Farles already Grey by nature, went ashen, his words tumbling out in a torrent of excuses he claimed that he had not sought this communication with Formby, but when approached he felt it his duty to explore anything that might put an end to the bloodshed, and in this spirit proposed that the Lord High Squirrel should meet with Formby's Envoy.

Now drenched with sweat and trembling with fear, Farles begged Cosmo that he might be permitted to sit in his presence. Cosmo indicated his assent by gesturing towards a small bale of Pinestraw, while he himself leaned back into his oversized "throne" and watched as Farles tried to sit on a bale which was clearly not big enough for the purpose. Cosmo was enjoying this.

DRESSED TO KILL

'I'm not sure that it suits me' said Adolphus Greyman as he tried on his prosthetic tail for the very first time. Surveying himself in a puddle he turned this way and that trying to get the best view, 'of course the colour's wrong, and I'm still not sure about the length.'

'Don't worry my Lord, the special rejuvenation shampoo that we are going to use on your coat will work equally well on the tail. As to your tail length, I think maybe we could shorten it a bit.'

Fixit Red the maker of false limbs and other such appendages, failed to see the irony of his offer to shorten Adolphus Greyman's tail, but it was not lost on Greyman who decided that on reflection by way of the puddle that "he could live with it."

The tail fitted, next came the rejuvenation shampoo. Greyman was puzzled at the extreme precautions that appeared to go with the application of the shampoo. Two white coated Squirrels wearing masks and carrying strangely marked containers, along with what appeared to be long handled paint brushes had entered into Fixit Red's shop. As they entered, Fixit Red showed a remarkable turn of paw for a Squirrel of his age and was gone in an instance.

The white coated Squirrels introduced themselves as Berk & Haire Fur Renovation Technicians , telling Greyman that he should not be alarmed by their appearance, as the process was really quite safe and that their protective clothing was just to protect them from any irritation that might arise from the constant use of the shampoo. For him, the process would be risk free, but could cause irritation to the eyes and to prevent this he should wear "these." Greyman was handed what had clearly once been a pair of human children's spectacles now heavily modified to act as goggles.

Donning these he stood ready, and with his new tail securely fitted uttered the fateful words, **'I am ready to be rejuvenated'**.

BECOMING GREY AGAIN !
(Sketch only - actual process classified)

With that, Berk and Haire opened their tins of "Shampoo" and set about Greyman with a vengeance. Their long-handled brushes clashing with each other as they scrubbed and shampooed Greyman from ear to his newly fitted tail.

The transformation was incredible and immediate. Gone was the decrepit nicotine stained tramp like figure, to be replaced by a glistening grey coated Squirrel.

Using the same puddle, he basked in its reflection, pronouncing, **'now I'm ready to return.'**

NEVER GO BACK

When Cosmo had been told that the Peace Envoy would be Adolphus Greyman, he had initially dismissed it out of hand, but had been prevailed upon by Ermin Grey and some other members of his inner circle to accede to the meeting.

Ermin Grey had been Cosmos long suffering wife, and had borne him multiple offspring, many of which had died in the ill-fated Battle of Wam Dyke Bridge. Initially it had been thought that Cosmo had married Ermin Grey on the rebound after his engagement to Pamilla Duchess of Nothing had fallen through, but the longevity of their relationship had surprised many in the Squirrel world.

Privately counselling against the invasion of Formby, she had been overruled by several of her sons who encouraged Cosmo to attack the Formby Colony. Only two of those sons had survived the battle, namely, Glaucous and Gunmetal, and now suitably chastened by their loss, they too had urged Cosmo to meet with Greyman, arguing "what harm could it do." **What harm indeed!**

GETTING THERE

Such was the security situation that existed in the "Bad Lands" between the borders of Formby and the Citadel of Holborn Hill, that just getting Greyman to the meeting had proved almost insurmountable. The Pine Marten predation had rendered the usual routes impassable; envoys had been sent to the Pine Martens to explore the possibility of safe passage, offering captured Grey Squirrels by way of an inducement to allow Greyman to get to Holborn Hill.

The envoys were never heard of again!

The decision to fly Greyman to Holborn Hill on the back of a Red Kite Milvus Bomber had been the last resort because it offered many pitfalls, not least Greyman's fear of flying, and his further fear that his tail would not be able to survive the turbulence of the flight.

Other factors being considered and unknown to Greyman:

1) Would the Shampoo coating survive the altitude?
2) What would be the security implications of letting the Greys see a Red Kite Milvus Bomber up close and personal.

Torben Red confirmed that as long as the Kite did not fly too fast the shampoo coating would remain intact, and that Greyman could be landed by night on a field close to the Citadel, thus preventing the Greys prying eyes gaining any intelligence as to the Milvus Bomber's capabilities.

Now there was only Greyman to convince.

Vermillion Red was at her persuasive best suggesting extra strapping would prevent his tail from flying off, and looking Greyman straight in the eye she said:

'Think how you left Holborn Hill... Mu-tailated, cast out into the Bad Lands to fend for yourself, hiding in ditches until you reached the sanctuary of Formby, enduring the terrible cruelty of the Nicotine Mines. You have endured all of that and now you have the chance to return, not as a broken down cripple, but as a great Peace Envoy, shaking paws with the Lord High Squirrel on equal terms, does that not compensate for a little air sickness?'

VERMILLION
RED

THE EMINENCE
'NOIR'

THE MEETING

Cosmo, after listening to his wife and the advice of his sons, did what Cosmo always did, he ignored it, and would not consider a meeting with Greyman, that is, until a survivor of the battle of Wam Dyke Bridge turned up at Holborn Hill.

Long thought to have perished, this trooper had escaped the waters of the ruptured canal that had killed so many of his comrades, and after months of attempts had finally managed to cross the Plains of Halsall by night to return to Holborn Hill.

This in itself was not unusual, as many such stragglers had returned in this manner, but it was the story that he brought with him that intrigued. He told of his time hiding in ditches and rabbit warrens trying not only to escape the Red soldiers, but also the human farmers that would shoot Greys dead on sight.

Listening to this tale was a member of the Intelligence Service the STAS (Special Tactical Assault Section), this was the part of the Grey Intelligence Service that reported directly to Ermin Grey and dealt with assassinations and counter insurgence.

On interviewing the soldier and initially thinking it was just another tale of Squirrel derring-do, his ears suddenly pricked up when the soldier began to tell of coming across a strange column of squirrels who were obviously prisoners chained together and carrying some sort of pack upon their backs. Following by the light of the moon, he watched them enter into what appeared to be a mine entrance built into a large sand dune. Further surveillance made difficult by the arrival of a group of The Kemel Noir, (the hereditary bodyguards of Kemel Red, all distinguishable by their black tails and black ear tufts), who, after donning "gas masks" threw what looked like pinecones into the mine entrance.

Wild shrieks and cries rang out from the mine and then a terrible silence, followed by a large thud as the front of the mine was totally enveloped by a huge collapse of sand from the dune above.

Any trace of the mine and the unfortunate prisoners now totally obliterated. The Kemel Noir removed their masks to survey their handywork and were heard to say, "**the Greys won't know what's hit them after we've used this stuff on them.**"

The Kemel Noir left as quickly as they came, almost treading upon the trooper as he lay face down in the scrub hoping for all that he was worth that he had not been noticed. Capture by the Kemel Noir would have been a fate worse than death their cruelty was legend. He thanked his "maker" as they passed him by and loped off into the night.

The STAS officer recited this story to his superior who retold it to Ermin Grey at their daily security meeting. For some time STAS had been collecting reports of strange activities in and around the area that the humans called Cabin Hill, but its proximity to the sea and it being in the remotest part of Formby, had made intelligence gathering extremely difficult.

From adding the soldier's story to other scraps of information gathered from captured Red prisoners, a picture was emerging, and it was a highly disturbing one. The Reds had developed a "Wonder Weapon" that would totally change the balance of power. So deadly was this weapon that any future conflict between the Reds and the Greys would end with the extermination of the Grey Squirrel.

When Cosmo was informed of the seriousness of the intelligence by Ermin Grey, he too became highly alarmed. If the Reds had such a weapon, it would only be a matter of time before they used it. Their own work on a chemical weapon which closely resembled the Red's P.C.P (Pine Cone Psychosis) program had stalled, and was nowhere near ready to be deployed on the battlefield.

Cosmo had to buy more time to redress the balance of power, so reluctantly, he made the fateful decision to meet the "Peace Envoy" Adolphus Greyman. The meeting was to be held in Cosmo's private apartments; Security, always heavy, now doubled by the STAS close protection troops that Ermin Grey had stationed on every entrance.

No one was to enter without a total body search, the only exceptions to this rule were Cosmo and Ermin Grey. Farles Duke of Noware was initially excluded from the proposed meeting with Greyman, but after he had protested that as heir to the throne it was his constitutional duty to represent Queen Doddery at any meeting with a representative of a foreign power, Cosmo finally agreed to his attendance so long as he was subjected to the same security procedures as everyone else. Farles protested that he should not be subjected to a full body search, as any such search would result in a member of the "working-class" laying hands on his "Royal Personage" and could not be countenanced as it infringed his "constitutional prerogative".

Cosmo had had enough saying, 'no search, no meeting,' before going on to remind Farles what had happened to the Speaker Wocreb when he had tried to discuss constitutional matters.

THE FLYING TROJAN
HORSE

Climbing a tree with a false tail was not for everyone, and when told that he would have to climb to the top of the tallest pine tree in Formby to get onboard the waiting Red Kite Milvus Bomber, Greyman refused point blank.

After heated discussions with the ground crew, it was decided that the Kite would land from the tree and Greyman could get on board for the flight to Holborn Hill.

Greyman's relief turned out to be short lived, as with a mighty whoosh of air the giant bird landed close to Greyman, the turbulence so great Greyman was knocked to the floor causing his tail to fall off!! Its lightweight construction made it easy prey to the coastal wind that had suddenly sprung up, causing the ground crew to engage in a frantic pursuit of the runaway tail.

Aided by the still freshening wind, the tail took on the characteristics of a child's toy kite, darting up and down back and forth it whizzed, until finally it was captured and reunited with the hapless Greyman.

Now there was another problem, the light. It had been planned that Greyman would be landed at dusk in a field behind Holborn Hill, but now it really was quite gloomy, and the Kite was not happy about landing in a strange field in the pitch black. More heated exchanges followed before the Kite reluctantly agreed to take Greyman to Holborn Hill.

Strapped into a specially constructed harness, Greyman had time to marvel at the sheer power of the Kite as it flapped its giant wings effortlessly as it lifted off into the night sky. The short flight passed uneventfully guided by a helpful moon, and soon the dark mass of Holborn Hill loomed into view. Overflying the fortress, the Kite landed without incident in a corn field.

Clambering free from his harness and making sure that his tail was fully secured, Greyman strode forward from under the protective wing of the Kite, to be met by a detachment of STAS soldiers who subjected him to a ferocious body search. No orifice was safe from their prying paws... even forcing him to remove his tail for their inspection! Now certain that he was not concealing any weapons or explosives, Greyman was escorted into Holborn Hill.

One worrying thought suddenly struck him, **why were there no arrangements for his return flight!!**

On entering the Fortress, Greyman was escorted straight to Cosmo's private apartments and then into the Conference Room. Sitting at the head of the long table was Cosmo the Lord High Squirrel of Great Britain, resplendent in his regalia of office and oozing confidence. Sat next to him Ermin Grey looked equally imposing, determined not to be outshone by Pamilla Duchess of Nothing, Ermin Grey was wearing a tiara that had once belonged to the Royal Family.

Completing the family picture, son Gunmetal stood dutifully behind his father. Mysteriously his brother Glaucous had gone down with a last-minute illness and was unable to attend the fateful meeting. (Conspiracy theorists would claim that he must have had prior knowledge of what was about to unfold).

Hoping to see some of his former comrades from the army high command, Greyman was stunned to see the army was now represented by cadets from the military academy.

Seated to their left and separated by some distance was Farles Duke of Noware and his family. At the very last minute Farles had insisted that he be allowed to bring his wife and daughters to the meeting. Cosmo had agreed they could attend, providing that they underwent the same security checks as every other attendee. Cosmo's thinking had been that Farles would not allow Pamilla Duchess of Nothing and her two gormless daughters Betawix and Eugenics to be subjected to the invasive body searches that the security precautions demanded.

Cosmo was wrong! Such was Farles ambition for his family he had also forced his mother Queen Doddery and father Prince Fillup to endure the security checks, and they too now sat at the table.

Ermin Grey was the first to speak.

'On behalf of Cosmo Marmajuke Grey Lord High Squirrel of Great Britain and the Isles, I welcome you.'

Greyman still standing, and without a chair, started to deliver his carefully rehearsed speech.

'I bring you an offer, the like of which has never been made in all the annals of Squirrel history. This is an offer of a total cessation of hostilities on all fronts, starting immediately. This will put an end to the war that has for so long divided our two great nations. Along with this peace proposal I have a further pledge from the Formby Republic, that they will accept Dominion status in the Greater Squirrel Republic that the merging of the two Republics will create, and furthermore, they will accept you Cosmo Marmajuke Grey, as the rightful Lord High Squirrel of all Britain and The Isles, and furthermore they would pledge their allegiance to you in perpetuity.'

The already febrile atmosphere was now supercharged by Greyman's speech. No one, including Cosmo had expected this. This was not an offer about peace talks, but a total capitulation to Cosmo's demands, he would now be able to bring the "Rebel Republic" under his control, his life's work would be vindicated.

Ignoring protocol, Cosmo jumped to his feet and embraced Greyman like a long lost friend. As he did so it occurred to him that Greyman's coat had a slightly tacky feel to it, but this thought was soon lost in an orgy of paw shaking and back slapping as all those seated at the table rose to shake Greyman's paw.

Even Farles and his ghastly family were not immune to the hysteria, forcing their way through to Greyman's side, they too embraced and congratulated him, assuring him that the Monarchy would do everything in its power to facilitate the momentous events that he proposed.

Vermillion Red had no way of knowing just how fast the coating on Adolphus Greyman's fur was melting, **but melting it was**, and as it did, it allowed the deadly toxin Nuttachoc secreted beneath, to enter the room.

Now released from the wax coating that had contained it, the Nuttachoc did its deadly work quietly and efficiently, there would be no escape from its lethal embrace. All those present in the room would soon succumb, some sooner than others. The bog eyed Princesses Betawix and Eugenics had exacerbated the speed of their demise by planting kisses on Greyman, hoping this show of affection would somehow advance their fathers claim for the Monarchy. They now lay writhing on the floor until death eased their torment.

Death was no respecter of rank or status, Cosmo followed almost immediately.

Soon only one bemused sole, Adolphus Greyman was left alive, unable to comprehend what had happened and feeling ill. The last thing he heard before succumbing to the Nuttachoc's icy embrace and before falling dead on top of Cosmo's lifeless corpse, was the slamming of doors.

In a matter of moments not a sound could be heard. All that entered that room lay dead, all victim to Vermillion Red's cunning. Her plan so meticulously thought out, had delivered beyond her wildest dreams. Using Greyman's vanity and self-importance she had convinced him along with a promise of a new tail, that she was working to overthrow Kemel Red and that Greyman should use his contacts in the Grey Peace Party to meet and explore a lasting Peace Agreement. This would come about after Vermillion Red, aided and abetted by Betterred, had staged a coup that would remove Kemel Red from power.

When her plan had been discovered by Kemel Red's Security Police, it had forced her to produce a master class of acting. Throwing herself at Kemel Red's feet, she claimed that there had been no plot to overthrow him, but it had been a necessary deception to convince Greyman to undertake the mission. Notwithstanding the above, her plan to turn Greyman into a "*chemical weapon*" was the real tour de force.

Kemel Red had wanted to use Nuttachoc in an all-out assault on Holborn Hill, but the misgivings of his War Minister Torben Red and his Propaganda Minister Gurballs Red, plus the risk of human interference, had stayed his paw. Vermillion Red's plan offered a chance to kill the Lord High Squirrel without the collateral damage of using Nuttachoc in large amounts, the only ones to be killed would be those attending the meeting.

Torben Red had developed a masking agent, that when painted onto the fur would allow the fur to be overpainted with Nuttachoc, and then treated with wax to seal in the deadly toxin. The masking agent would protect the unfortunate recipient long enough so that he could travel to the meeting without showing any ill effects. Once at the meeting and given the abnormally high temperatures that Cosmos private apartments experienced, the wax would very soon start to melt, and this would release the toxin to do its deadly work, even its unwitting carrier would no longer be safe from its catastrophic effects.

News slowly filtered out of Holborn Hill across the "Bad Lands" of Halsall and on into "The Viking Republic of Formby," of a great disaster that had befallen the Lord High Squirrel, his Ministers, Army Chiefs, Queen Doddery, Prince Fillup and Farles Duke of Noware and his family. All had been killed by what had been thought to be a gas leak.

Gurballs Red addressing the crowds that had gathered outside the Ministry of Constant Truth declared:

'Let this day stand testament to all those who would seek to destroy us. We will not sit here quaking with fear while you skulk behind your fortress walls plotting to destroy us, we will reach out and strike you down. We have "cut off the head of the *snake*, but the body still lives." Only one "*Being*" can save us from its lethal convulsions, the Supreme "*Being*" that is Kemel Red!'

And suddenly there he was, The Supreme Leader in all his glory, paw in paw with Vermillion Red.

Rarely seen in public, the Supreme Leader was met with wild cheering, chanting and chaos as the crowd surged forward hoping to get closer to his "divine presence". So great was the force of the crowd that even the Supreme Leader's bodyguards, the Kemel Noir, could no longer hold them back.

The decision was taken by Gurballs Red to deploy the Revernants. Freed from the duties of running the now closed Nicotine Mines, they had been turned into a crowd control unit. The Revernants set about the crowd with such ferocity that previous good humour now turned to fear, and pandemonium ensued as the baton whirling Revernants tore into the crowd.

Gurballs Red's propaganda "triumph" was now a disaster and Kemel Red wanted no part of it. Gathering Vermillion Red to his side and flanked by his bodyguards, he rounded on his hapless Propaganda Minister saying.

'I hold you personally responsible for this debacle.'

Vermillion Red, a smile flickering across her face, whispered, sarcastically, almost hissing into Gurballs Red's ear,

'That went well.'

before leaving paw in paw with the Supreme Leader.

Vermillion Red the "The Eminence Rouge" was back where she belonged.

Riding a tiger is easy, getting off is the hard part......

I GLAUCOUS

To lose one member of your family could be said to be a tragedy, but when you lose everyone related to you and a few more besides, it could be seen as an advantage!

Glaucous Grey, the last surviving scion of the ruling Grey Squirrel dynasty, was very lucky. A *mysterious illness* had prevented him from attending the *Peace Conference* that had resulted in the deaths of his father Manyshades Grey, the Lord High Squirrel of Great Britain and the Isles, his mother Ermin and also his brother Gunmetal. Also killed at this *Peace Conference* were Farles Duke of Noware and his ghastly wife Pamilla Duchess of Nothing and progeny, along with the onetime leader of the Grey Army of the North, Adolphus Greyman. In short, anyone who was anyone in the Grey Squirrel world and a few more besides, were now dead.

Glaucous was roused from his sick bed to be told of the events that had unfolded. When it became clear to the STAS troops (Squirrel Tactical Assault Squad) guarding the conference that something was going terribly wrong, they had slammed the doors to the meeting hall, effectively entombing all those inside.

News of the disaster spread far and wide. In the breakaway Red Squirrel Republic of Formby, wild scenes of jubilation had greeted the news, and a public holiday proclaimed to celebrate the event. Kemel Red the Republic's seldom seen in public *Supreme Leader*, made a surprise appearance at the Ministry of Constant Truth. His very appearance had caused a riot forcing Gurballs Red the Propaganda Minister to unleash the *Revernants* (former Nicotine Mine guards hated by one and all) upon the over exuberant crowd in an attempt to regain order.

None of this was known to Glaucous as intelligence gathering in Formby was at best problematic, and in reality, virtually impossible, due to the paranoid nature of the regime. Glaucous immediately concluded that Kemel Red's breakaway Republic was responsible for the outrage, that had made an orphan of him, but he had much more important things to deal with, Formby would have to wait.

Glaucous was swiftly installed as the new Lord High Squirrel in a ceremony that lasted all of a minute. His installation had been at the behest of the commander of the STAS, Comodus Grey who told Glaucous in no uncertain manner 'if you don't do it, we'll find someone else who will.' Comodus a student of ancient Rome also decided from here on in that the STAS troops that he commanded would now be known as the SPG (Squirrel Pretorian Guard).

MARRY OR DIE

Glaucous, now the Lord High Squirrel, had rejected Comodus' offer to make him an Emperor by saying the two million Grey Squirrels living in Great Britain would expect a fair and firm leadership, and that would have to involve a partnership between him and the monarchy which would not be best served by him being crowned as an Emperor. Comodus was unimpressed by this argument but was persuaded to delay any enthronement for the moment "until the dust settled."

Glaucous now had a real problem, what little he knew of history (*squirrel history being oral and much subjected to distortion through constant repetition*) told him being an Emperor usually ended badly.

So, after much deliberation he came up with a plan. He needed to get married into the monarchy to legitimise his regime, the problem being that all of the main members of the Royal Family had been killed. The only surviving member was Grand Duchess Anaesthesia a second cousin of Deadwood the Eighth, the King that had been forced to abdicate when Glaucous' grandfather Manyshades Grey had seized power and installed himself as Lord High Squirrel.

Initial enquiries revealed that Grand Duchess Anaesthesia had married Max Von Batenball, the brother of Elisabeth Bowline, this union produced three daughters Megalomania, Euthanasia, and Betamax. Further inquiries revealed that Betamax had recently declared herself to be in a relationship with a transgender Red Squirrel, the subsequent furore had forced her to go into hiding, leaving either Euthanasia or Megalomania as the candidates for his marital aspirations.

WHICH ONE TO CHOOSE

In truth it mattered very little which one of the sisters he married, as both were members of the Royal Family. By marrying either would give his regime and his family name the dynastic legitimacy he so badly craved.

For appearance' sake he met them both together and was immediately struck by how unalike they were. Euthanasia was large by squirrel standards, with large protruding front teeth and large bulging eyes, while Megalomania was the embodiment of femininity, sleek grey from her head to her toes she exuded sexuality.

The choice was not a difficult one to make, he chose Euthanasia for his wife, despite his overwhelming attraction to Megalomania, he reasoned that she was **trouble with a capital T**, and would not be prepared to play a supportive role as a dutiful wife, but would insist on a marriage of equals, thus ruling her out of consideration despite her obvious attractiveness.

Euthanasia however was just what he needed, she lacked confidence, had no interests other than eating and drinking and would do whatever Glaucous told her to. Within the hour they were married and the following day at the insistence of the Squirrel Pretorian Guard, urged on by its Commander Comodus, Glaucous was made Emperor.

At the enthronement he had promised to avenge the death of his father Cosmo Marmajuke Grey and all the others killed by the chemical weapon Nuttachoc, laying the blame firmly on the breakaway Red Squirrel Republic of Formby, saying this cowardly attack under the guise of a *peace conference* had proved once and for all there could be no dialogue with a regime that would sink to such depths of depravity.

Furthermore, only the complete and utter annihilation of the Formby Republic and its Red Squirrel population would compensate for the heinous crime that had been inflicted on the Grey Squirrel world.

BITING THE HAND
THAT FEEDS

Brian Betwetter was an apparatchik not to any political party, but to the National Trust, the quango that runs the Red Squirrel Reserve in Formby, his devotion to the Trust was akin to religious fervour.

Bespectacled, slightly unworldly, and taken to wearing shorts and sandals in the middle of winter and married to a former nun, he took his job as Warden of the Reserve very seriously. Indeed, it had been his idea to implement the *shoot to kill* policy that had cost countless Grey Squirrels their lives in the *total exclusion zone* that surrounded the Formby Reserve, so that when news was brought to him about a dog on a lead being beaten up by a gang of squirrels carrying staves of wood and wielding them like baseball bats, he immediately thought that his total exclusion zone must have breached by the Greys, but whilst interviewing the unfortunate child who's dog had been attacked, he was stunned to hear that the perpetrators were not Grey but **Red,** Brian was horrified! The Red Squirrel Reserve at Formby was one of the National Trust's biggest earners, thousands flocked to the reserve each weekend.

Brian had to act and act fast. He immediately implemented a total embargo on any discussion of the event, buying the child's parents silence with the promise of free firewood for life. The unfortunate victim, a pug called Eric was not so lucky; the hurriedly summoned Trust-supporting vet concluded that in forty years of veterinary practice he had never seen such brutality, and despite his best efforts Eric succumbed to his injuries, leaving his owner Calista, a precocious brat if there ever was one, inconsolable.

A REVERNANT

THE BLAME GAME

In Red Squirrel households only one topic of conversation could be heard above the crunching of nuts was.. *who carried out the attack*? Soon the blame was laid firmly at the door of the Revernants, these former Nicotine Mine guards had taken to roaming the Reserve looking for trouble, and this attack was just one in a long list of provocations that included biting the fingers of the human children as they held out peanuts to be nibbled, refusing to pose for selfies, along with defecating and urinating on visitors from the surrounding trees. Something would have to be done or that carefully choreographed relationship with the humans and the protection this relationship afforded, would be lost.

Brian Betwetter saw the same problem... in a nutshell... visitors to the Reserve wanted to bring their children and pets to walk in the woods and watch the pretty Red Squirrels play, and his *shoot to kill, total exclusion zone*, coupled with a bounty paid to local farmers for killing Grey Squirrels had made Formby into a paradise for the Reds. So why were they now biting the hand that fed them?

Brian pondered this conundrum with a new vigour as an email announced the forthcoming visit of a member of the Royal Family to the Reserve. The National Trust actively sought the patronage of Royals however minor, but in the case of the Countess of Parbold they were *really scraping the bottom of the barrel*! Once married to a third cousin of some non-entity distantly related to the Royal Family, she had insisted on being ennobled as her price for leaving the marriage without too much fuss.

Visiting Formby in her newly acquired role of a *distinguished patron* would be her first *Royal* visit and she was determined to make the most of it.

WHAT TO DO
ABOUT THE BODIES

Being an Emperor wasn't all it was cracked up to be, especially when it came to living accommodation. Glaucus' father Cosmo's luxury staterooms had been quarantined since the mass poisoning, depriving Glaucous of accommodation worthy of an Emperor, but for no more. The trouble was no one could say with any degree of certainty that the lethal Nuttachoc virus was not still active in the sealed off rooms.

Comodus liked to think of himself as a problem solver, and his solution to the Nuttachoc problem was to unseal one of the doors and chuck a Pine Marten in, close the door again and go back in a few days to see if the unfortunate animal had survived or not. The Pine Marten already under sentence of death for barbequing squirrels would be no great loss.

Glaucous liked this plan very much and ordered it be carried out immediately. The Pine Marten was duly inserted and left entombed. Some three days later squirrels from Pawmandown wearing breathing apparatus fashioned out of an old snorkel, and chemical warfare suits made out of bin liners, apprehensively opened the State Room doors to be greeted by a very healthy if somewhat hungry Pine Marten telling them.

'I could murder a Squirrel Kebab!'

Glaucous watched the removal of the bodies of his parents from a safe distance, despite being told by the Chemical Weapons Team in attendance, that tests had revealed no surviving trace of the virus.

Determined that his parents be accorded a funeral that befitted their status, he ordered that a great funeral pyre be built so all of the bodies could be consumed and cleansed by the power of the flame, but as everywhere was so wet, he had them thrown down a mine shaft instead!!!

HOW TO OCCUPY YOUR TIME WHEN YOU'RE A GOD!

Kemel Red the Supreme Leader of the break-away Red Squirrel Republic of Formby and self-proclaimed God, when not communing with the Universe and pondering the unfathomable, liked to drink. Since the great success of the mass poisoning of the *Grey hierarchy* his consumption of Pinecone Brandy had increased dramatically, leaving him visibly unsteady on his paws. Old by squirrel standards he was beginning to lose it, and was becoming more and more dependent on Vermillion Red his half-sister to run the Republic, and it was she that convened the emergency meeting of the Total Security Council to deal with *the Revernants problem*.

Addressing the Council which consisted of Gurballs Red (Propaganda Minister), Torben Red (War Minister), and Betterred (Internal Security Minister), Vermillion Red demanded to know what was being done about the Revernants! Betterred said that the problem of the Revernants was not one that could be easily solved, as though they were deeply unpopular with rank and file squirrels, large swathes of the army were broadly sympathetic to their bad behaviour and any moves to discipline them could cause a dangerous rift between the leadership and the Army.

Vermillion Red was having none of this.

So we sit back and do nothing as a gang of renegade Nicotine Mine guards destroy our carefully cultivated relationship with the humans! Does the Propaganda Minister have nothing to say? After all, are they not his creatures?'

It had been Gurballs Red's decision to redeploy the Revernants from running the now closed Nicotine Mines into a paramilitary force that could be used ostensibly for crowd control. In reality, he saw them as a counterweight to the Kemel Noir (the Blacks) the regime's hereditary bodyguards, in the forthcoming succession struggle, and he was not going to give them up because some dog had come to a sticky end.

Betterred sensed the looming confrontation, the animus between Vermillion Red and the Propaganda Minister was legend and it was now threating to boil over.

Trying to defuse the situation he said.

'The continuation of the Republic depends on the humans. Like them or loath them we must continue to engage with them if we are to survive, our recent victory on the battlefield at Wam Dyke Bridge and our successful chemical assault on Holborn Hill have bought us time, but the basic facts remain.... the Greys outnumber us 200/1 and without the humans we are lost!'

Gurballs Red was having none of this.

'This kind of defeatist talk will not cover up for the fact the humans need us just as much as we need them, look at that huge Visitor Centre they have just built, without us there would be no Formby Reserve. They have taken us for granted for too long and maybe it's time we reminded them just who's in charge!'

THE VISIT

The necessity for the Countess of Parbold's visit to Formby was to open the brand-new Red Squirrel Visitor Centre built at great expense by the National Trust to showcase the Red Squirrels to a wider world. Wildly overbudget because of unstable ground conditions, and the enforced relocation of a colony of Natterjack toads, this edifice needed cash paying visitors and fast.

The choice of the Countess of Parbold to open it had been necessitated by lack of funds, her main attraction had been that she lived nearby, and she was cheap. Although she, saw it in entirely different way, in her mind it was the first of many *things* that she would be called upon to open, culminating in *the opening of a Hospital*, and a few recalcitrant Red Squirrels were not going to deflect her from her dream. So, when she was told that it would be best if she cancelled her planned walkabout in the woods because of security concerns, she refused point blank. Svetlana Simpkins aka The Countess of Parbold **would not be deterred**, *the "Visit"* would go on as planned, come what may.

NEW RECRUITS

While the Reds argued about their "*special relationship*" with the humans, Emperor Glaucous continued to assert his control on Britain's Grey Squirrel population. Runners were sent the length and breadth of the Country to announce the enthronement of Emperor Glaucous, along with the biggest ever recruitment drive to replenish the army so badly depleted by the Wam Dyke Bridge defeat.

Soon Holborn Hill was bursting at the seams with eager recruits, their numbers far exceeded Glaucous' expectations and this gave him an immediate problem: he had hoped to have time to train and discipline the recruits into a unified fighting force capable of defeating the highly organised Red Army, but the sheer numbers arriving daily could not be fed, never mind trained!

The decision to close the gates of Holborn Hill was not taken lightly, but the Fortress was running out of food, and with winter approaching fast, the danger of famine now loomed large. It had been Comodus' decision to shut the gates, saying.

'If we let that lot in there won't be enough for us.'

Originally hailing from Yorkshire, and always the altruist, he addressed the masses outside from the battlements telling them to

'bugger off and come back in spring.'

Unable to enter the Fortress, large numbers of would be recruits were forced to forage for food in an increasingly hostile countryside. Their sheer numbers had provided local farmers already battling financial ruin because of the incessant wet weather with an unexpected lifeline.

The National Trust doubled the bounty they paid for dead Grey Squirrels. The effects were dramatic, gone were the sullen farmers sitting on their tractors bemoaning the weather. Now shooting parties were the thing, the countryside resounded with gunfire from morning till dark. Week after week went by, no copse was safe from a farmer with a shotgun blasting anything that vaguely resembled a Grey Squirrel. This carnage was not only inflicted on squirrels, the local hospital had to open a closed ward to deal with gunshot wounds caused by farmers mistakenly firing on each other in their relentless pursuit of the National Trust bounty, it had to stop, and as always, money was at the bottom of it.

The money paid out by the National Trust in the form of 'blood money' to the farmers now exceeded the total income from the Formby Reserve. This coupled with the sheer extravagance of the recently completed, and soon to be opened, Visitor Centre was decimating the Trusts income to such an extent, that there really was no option... The bounty for dead Grey Squirrels would have to cease immediately, whatever the consequences.

When this decision was relayed to Brian Betwetter at the Formby Reserve he was horrified. The loss of his *shoot to kill* policy was a major blow to his counter insurgency strategy, and despite his protestations that not culling the Greys would threaten the Red population, and the long term viability of the Visitor centre could be imperilled, he was overruled and told to notify the farmers of the cancellation of the bounty forthwith.

That night sitting in the kitchen of his timber framed cabin adjoining the Formby Reserve, Brian confided his misgivings to his long serving wife Conchita, formerly Sister Perpetual Indulgence, (she had left Holy Orders to join Brian in his life's vocation, the preservation of the Red Squirrel in Formby).

Fiercely loyal to Brian she railed against the Trust, saying.

'Their penny pinching was endangering his life's work.'

Always the apparatchik, he counselled his wife that at least they hadn't cancelled his robotic tree planters.

THE REVERNANTS

After the dog incident, the Revernants had expected a backlash from the Red leadership: Gurballs Red had factored this into his calculations when he secretly ordered the Revernants Commander, Bahstado to carry out the attack.

Gurballs Red knew that change was coming to the Formby Republic. Kemel Red's days as Supreme Leader were numbered, age and alcohol had rendered him no longer able to control events. Plots were everywhere, cousins, brothers, half-brothers all schemed to replace The Leader, but it was the sister that concerned him most. That sister was Vermillion Red, her visceral dislike of him meant that if she became The Leader he would be exiled at best but more probably, he would meet with an accident from which he would not recover.

He needed a crisis which he could turn to his advantage and the Revernants were well placed to provoke such a crisis.

Summoning Bahstado, ostensibly the purpose of the meeting was to deliver a stern reprimand on behalf of the leadership for the dog attack, and to warn the Revernants as to their future conduct, but Gurballs Red had other ideas; he delivered not a reprimand but an order to Bahstado to break into the outbuildings of the newly built Visitor Centre and '*do some damage.*'

He had considered breaking into the Centre itself, but having been designed with security in mind it would have presented a formidable challenge, however the outbuildings holding the machinery would be a much easier target, so he instructed Bahstado *to seek out any machinery stored there and give the wiring a* ***'real good chewing.'***

IGNORANCE IS BLISS UNLESS FOLLOWED BY FOLLY

Finally, the great day dawned. The opening of the Visitor Centre had been timed to coincide with the Spring Bank Holiday to facilitate the maximum number of visitors and had been Brian Betwetter's decision; the opening was his "*baby*," and nothing was going to be left to chance. Every aspect of the opening had been run through time and time again, there was to be no deviation from Brian's plan, all the big wigs from the National Trust were going to be there along with a camera crew from the BBC to record the event.

At exactly 6.37 on the morning of the opening, Brian made a decision that would haunt him for the rest of his days. He decided that the Countess of Parbold's tree planting ceremony should be done not the traditional way with a spade, but by using one of the newly delivered robotic tree planters currently residing in the outbuildings.

Quickly the idea expanded, why use one when all ten of them could be just as easily lined up opposite the carpark, thereby emphasizing the Trust's commitment to lowering their carbon footprint by planting vast numbers of trees.

The planting of trees being necessary to prevent the giant sandhills moving inshore and engulfing the Reserve. This would not have been needed had the Trust (egged on by Brian), not decided on a policy of cutting down the trees in the first place in a misguided effort to make it "a better place for Natterjack Toads to live!" It had been Brian who finally realising the folly of this plan had persuaded the Trust to reverse its position and invest in the robotic tree planters.

Not trusting any of his staff, Brian unlocked the outbuilding and stood for a moment gazing in awe at his ten robotic Titans. The Atlas 347 was a fully electric, remote controlled, self-loading, driverless, automatic tree planter, and designed to be operated by a single hand control. Brian trembled in anticipation as he pressed the control button... nothing happened... pressing it again, still nothing.... finally, at the third time of asking the leading Titan lumbered forward in answer to Brian's ever more impatient commands.

This should have been the moment the normally cautious Brian abandoned the idea of using the robots, but a feeling of euphoria had empowered him to an unfamiliar boldness, dismissing the robot's initial lack of response as *newness,* and, heartened by the subsequent control he now exorcised over his charges, he had them lined up in a perfect phalanx facing the carpark. **By 7.05 am Brian's fate had been sealed.**

DOES ANYONE KNOW A DENTIST?

Bahstado was not looking forward to his meeting with Gurballs Red. Breaking into the outbuildings had been a doddle but the machinery inside proved impossible to damage. Despite their best efforts the Revernants could not chew through the armoured conduits that protected the tree planters wiring. The Atlas 347 had been designed to be virtually indestructible and it was living up to its billing.

As dawn broke it became clear just how strenuous their efforts had been, two of the Revernants had lost teeth and nearly all of them had bloodied gums!

Finally, Bahstado called the operation off despite one of his best chewers, Muncher, claiming to have 'got through to the wiring!'

Gurballs Red listened to Bahstado's report with mixed emotions, disappointed that the Revernants had failed in their attempted vandalism but heartened by the slavish devotion that the Revernants expressed to his cause. They indeed would be a powerful weapon in the looming leadership struggle.

WHEN THE BODY COUNT GETS TOO GREAT, STOP COUNTING

Comodus and the Pretorian Guard had a quiet winter safely ensconced in the Holborn Hill Fortress, not for them the privations of the countryside, though there were periods when the sound of gunfire would occasionally rouse them from their slumbers.

The return of spring brought a return of the would-be army recruits. Their number greatly diminished by the farmer's predation; they were soon absorbed into the army as replacements for those lost at Wam Dyke Bridge.

Glaucous his dynasty established by the birth of Eros, Mars and Phobos from his union with Betamax, now felt strong enough to turn his attention back to Formby.

The Nuttachoc attack had left no visible legacy, but in the Grey Squirrel collective psyche, the wounds ran deep. Their sense of shared invincibility by virtue of superior numbers now shattered by events, they would have to be far more cautious in their dealings with the breakaway Formby Republic.

Now residing in his father Manyshades Grey's decontaminated quarters and sitting on the very throne that his father had ordered the ill-fated invasion of Formby from, Glaucous listened as Comodus gave him his daily security briefing:

> *'The situation in the countryside had been stabilised by virtue of the fact that the farmers no longer seemed interested in shooting Grey Squirrels, why they've stopped we don't know, but we're right glad they have.'*

Comodus further stated that the army was back up to strength and in a position to launch another attack on Formby, should it be required. Breaking with protocol, Comodus in his gruff Yorkshire manner continued

'I wouldn't be bothered with the buggers, there's bugger all in Formby worth having! It's all sandhills and Natterjack toads, slimy little buggers they are, why don't we just leave them to it?'

Glaucous snapped

'It's our patriotic duty to avenge the death of our Leader and so many members of the Royal Family we can't just pretend it didn't happen, what kind of message would that send to our enemies?'

'I hear what you're saying your Majesty, but it didn't work out too well last time did it, and now the buggers have chemical weapons, along with an air force. Our superior numbers might not be enough for us to prevail, and for that reason me and the lads don't fancy it!'

"*Me and the lads*" was parlance for The Pretorian Guard. Glaucous was Emperor but in reality the Guard led by Comodus were the real power in the Land and they had little appetite for military expeditions when things were going so nicely for them in Holborn Hill.

Glaucous screamed

'I am the Emperor and I demand that the army is readied to attack Formby.'

Comodus in his most condescending manner intoned

'May I remind your Majesty just who made him Emperor in first place, it were us, without us thou's nowt, so forget Formby, those little Red buggers are too clever by half, they'll do for the'selves in time, just you mark my words. You stick to playing happy families with the missus, me and the lads will look after country, don't you fret your sen about it.'

THAT WASN'T
SUPPOSED TO
HAPPEN

The Countess of Parbold had been practising her "*royal wave*" for weeks, so hard had she practised, she now felt unable to lift her arm without the aid of prescription drugs, which she had been taking in ever increasing amounts. Now as her motorcade swept into the Formby Reserve she was is Squirrel parlance "*out of her Tree*". This fact was not lost on her fellow passenger Ghastlena Gristlethorpe, Chairperson Emeritus of the National Trust, who would testify at the subsequent inquest that the Countess of Parbold in her opinion 'had totally lost it.'

Reaching the gleaming new Visitor Centre, one could not fail to be impressed by its grandeur. The timber frame had been sourced from the trees cut down to make way for the Natterjack Toad's breeding pools. This frame had then been clad in hand beaten sheets of acid etched copper (this had been done despite police advice, that the proximity of Liverpool made the choice of copper a security risk). The building was surmounted by a thatched roof into which the thatcher had cut a giant figure of a Red Squirrel. The choice of a thatched roof had been one of the reasons that the Visitor Centre had gone so far over budget, but the renowned Japanese architect Footo Imoutho who had designed the Visitor Centre had insisted that the thatched roof, specially imported from Norfolk, encapsulated the fusion of "Earth to Sky" and had threatened to withdraw from the project if the Trust failed to deliver his vision in its entirety. The Trust had reluctantly acceded to his demands in a desperate attempt to finish the job and get some revenue flowing into the Trusts vastly depleted coffers.

As the Limousine pulled up, the first to alight was the Countess of Parbold. Ignoring Brian's outstretched hand of welcome she rushed into the centre, demanding 'where's the toilet,' somewhat confusing the assembled "worthies" who had been lined up for a meet-and-greet session. When the Countess finally reappeared, she offered the excuse 'sorry about that, my bladder's not what it was.'

Brian strode forward.

'Welcome your Royal Highness.'

By use of the title "Your Royal Highness" Brian had instantly elevated the Countess well beyond her status, and in doing so had endeared himself to her for life.

Complimenting Brian on his thigh length socks emblazoned with the National Trust Logo, the Countess was amazed when Brian told her that the socks had been made by his wife Conchita (formally Sister Perpetual Indulgence) out of one of her Wimples. Continuing in the spirit of the newly established bonhomie, the Countess asked Brian if they could skip the tree planting ceremony as her arm was "knackered" and she didn't think she could manage the spade. When Brian informed her that the he proposed to use one of his robotic tree planters to carry out the ceremony she positively beamed.

A VIEW FROM
THE TREES

All this activity was watched from the trees by the Revernants with a sense of growing anger, nothing the humans did surprised them, to Bhastado and his fellow Revernants, the Visitor Centre was one human intrusion into their world too many and something would have to be done about it.

The problem was the Red Squirrels themselves, years of performing tricks for peanuts provided by the humans had numbed their sense of self-worth to such a degree they no longer realised they had become no more than exhibits in zoo, and they were now only too happy to play out their part in the charade that was the Formby Reserve.

THE BEST LAID PLANS OF SQUIRRELS AND BRIAN

'Come this way your Royal Highness,' Brian ushered the Countess to stand next to the Atlas 347 that he had decided to use for the tree planting ceremony. Each machine had a designated number from one to ten, Brian chose number seven because he regarded it as his lucky number, further confirmed by the fact he had met his wife Conchita at a Seventh-day Adventist Open Day. This made the choice of number seven in Brian's mind a "no brainer," handing the Countess the remote control and telling her,

It's all pre-programmed and ready to go your Royal Highness, just press the big button.'

Grabbing the control with her good arm, she pressed the button as instructed. The machine roared into life swinging its telescopic digging and grabbing arm and extending it so that it was now directly above a piece of ground marked with a big white cross, using its pre-planned programming it proceeded to dig the hole for the tree planting ceremony.

Brian beamed as in no time at all, a perfectly round, if not a rather deep hole, now replaced the area marked with the white cross. What happened next would be regarded as the National Trust's "darkest hour" and would live long in the annuls of infamy. Instead of using its telescopic grabbing arm to pick up a potted sapling from the rear of the machine, it chose to grasp the Countess around the waist before turning her upside down in mid-air and then inserting her into the freshly dug hole. **The screams of the assembled worthies did not stop the machine as it proceeded to entomb the Countess with the previously excavated soil, soon there was no trace of the hole or the Countess!**

A TREE PLANTING CEREMONY GOES TRAGICALLY WRONG

Brian stood transfixed like a rabbit in the head-lights, until his brain finally regained control of his body, his cries of '**stay calm**' had little effect on the already fleeing worthies who had been forced into running for their lives by the collective lurch into life of the other nine robotic tree planters, moving initially forward as if guided by an unseen hand. (*The inquest jury would be told that it was possible that the robots were inadvertently under the control of the entombed Countess, who had been buried still clutching the remote control)!*

The first obstacles encountered by the phalanx of tree planters were the rows of parked cars neatly lined up in the newly resurfaced carpark. No.9 struck the first blow, encountering the Mayoral limousine, it struck a fearsome blow which punched a perfectly cylindrical hole though the bonnet, before neatly filling the hole with a potted sapling.

The Atlas 347 had been designed to carry fifteen pre-potted saplings at any one time and could, by way of a self-pulled trailer, carry an additional twenty saplings. It had been Brian's decision to load all ten tree planters with their full complement of saplings, despite only needing one for the actual ceremony, he had decided that the sight of the fully loaded tree planters would add a sense of theatre to the proceedings and thereby could not fail to enhance the visitor experience.

With hindsight, Brian's decision to showcase one of the planters towing the additional twenty-sapling trailer proved to be his ultimate undoing, as No.6 broke ranks and proceeded to assault a Hot Dog Van with a frenzied attack of hole punching and sapling planting. All thirty-five saplings were punched into the fabric of the van to such an extent that what had been a Hot Dog Van now resembled a small copse of trees so profuse were the saplings projecting from it!

The unfortunate Hot Dog vendor did not survive the attack. His last words were said to be 'do you want onions with that' before succumbing to a Pinus Sylvestris sapling through the heart.

GINO'S **HOT DOGS** **DRINKS**

DO YOU WANT ONIONS WITH THAT??.......

Some visitors had attempted to flee from the carnage in their cars, but the carpark had been designed so that cars could only enter and exit one at a time, therefore when No.3 positioned itself across the exit and lifted its arm in the manner of a striking scorpion, the visitors simply jumped out of their cars and ran into the woods screaming.

LAUGH - I NEARLY FELL OUT OF THE TREE

Bahstado and his fellow Revernants could not control their glee at the disaster that was unfolding beneath their elevated position. From the tops of the trees they had a bird's eye view as the showpiece opening of the Centre went from bad to worse, causing all the visitors to flee for their lives screaming and shouting.

The No.4 Tree Planter was the first to break rank by turning one hundred and eighty degrees and unleashing a ferocious assault on the Visitor Centre's front doors. These had been locked in anticipation of the Countess of Parbold opening them with a "Golden Key." *The key wasn't real gold. Brian had sprayed it with a car aerosol saying 'a golden day deserved a golden key.'*

The Visitor Centre's doors had been designed to be vandal-proof, but they were no match for an enraged Atlas 347 which simply smashed straight through them and into the building. What happened next would be the basis of a legal case that would bring the Trust to its knees.

Now firmly inside, No.4 began punching holes in everything. Computer screens exploded, counters collapsed under the weight of the assault, in an orgy of vandalism who would have thought one blow mattered more than another, but to the Trust's Insurers (Yokahama Mutual) the next blow struck would be the reason that they refused to pay the subsequent multimillion pound Insurance Claim. The blow that struck Brian's gold aerosol canister caused a spark which ignited its contents, turning it into a flame thrower which started the fire that eventually broke through to the thatched roof covering the Centre, completely destroying it in the process.

Yokahama's subsequent refusal to pay, hinged on one thing only, the Terms of the Insurance, cover specifically stipulated *no spirits or hazardous substances could be stored or left in the Centre at any time*. Brian after spraying the "Golden Key" had without thinking placed the aerosol in a drawer in the now demolished counter, meaning to collect it later. That it had been found by the rampant Atlas 347 and turned into an incendiary device was just bad luck. But to Yokahama Mutual, there was no such thing as "*bad luck*," just a badly written Policy, and this Policy unlike the Visitor Centre's roof, by now a smouldering ruin, was watertight, the subsequent Fire Brigade investigation found the aerosol and concluded **it** had been the reason for the fire.

The Fire Brigade had been called by the Captain of the MV Galapagos outward bound from Liverpool to Valparaiso. Captain Gomes having just dropped off the Pilot at Formby Point and was just taking a last look at the Formby shore before many days at sea, when his eye was taken to a fast-rising pall of smoke emanating from the Formby shore. So fast was the smoke billowing upwards, Captain Gomez (ironically an honorary member of the National Trust,) knew something was seriously wrong. Captain Gomez' call to the Coastguard Station was the first to raise the alarm about the burning Visitor Centre.

As people ran for their lives desperately dialling 999 on their mobile phones at the outset of the disaster, none of them were able to get through because of lack of a signal. The Reserve known to the locals as the "Bermuda Triangle" had long been involved in a dispute with telecoms providers who wished to erect a communications mast that would remove the communications blackout from the area. But true to form, the National Trust baulked and prevaricated at every design submitted to them for the mast.

With the opening of the Visitor Centre looming, the telecoms providers gave it their best shot, submitting a mast design so tree like, it was virtually impossible to detect when set amidst the trees on the Reserve. Given the urgency of the opening they had shipped the mast to Formby in advance of any agreement, certain that the National Trust would approve. **Wrong!** When Brian saw the mast, he immediately informed the not yet retired Trust's Chairperson, Ghastlena Gristlethorpe that the proposed mast was a desecration, a blot on the landscape, an infamy beyond infamy, a complete repudiation of all the Trust stood for. Hearing this from her "man on the spot", Ghastlena had refused to allow the mast's erection until after the opening.

When told that failure to erect the mast would mean visitors would not be able to use their mobile phones, Ghastlena was quoted as saying *it's hardly a matter of life or death is it*!!!

THE REVERNANT'S REVENGE

LOST REPUTATIONS
AND THE END
OF A DREAM

What a momentous day it had been. The Visitor Centre, the Jewel in the National Trust's crown, lay a smouldering ruin. The carpark resembled the outskirts of 1943 Stalingrad. Only now that the Emergency services had been able to clear the access road, was the true extent of the disaster revealed. *As far as the eye could see, cars lay slain where proud owners had eagerly parked them in anticipation of the "Grand Opening."*

Brian had fled the scene the moment that No 4 smashed through the Visitor Centre's front doors. His total dereliction of duty surprised everybody that knew him. Colleagues described him as having the National Trust in his DNA and could only speculate that he must have had a *"spiritual meltdown"* which caused him to flee, when he was needed the most.

Negotiating the carpark carnage on his solar

powered scooter, Brian arrived at the log cabin he shared with Conchita just as she was putting out the washing. Strangely, Conchita was wearing her Nun's attire, wimple and all. Answering Brian's puzzled look, she declared

'I always wear this when I put the washing out, I suppose it's just a habit I've grown into.'

Ignoring her explanation, Brian told Conchita to 'pack the suitcase were off, it's all gone tits up at Visitor centre and it's all my fault.'

So ended the career of the Red Squirrel's greatest defender. Brian had arrived in Formby a spotty faced teenager on an old motor bike full of conservationist zeal, determined to make a difference. Now twenty-five years later it was over, his dream slain by a toxic miasma of hubris and self-delusion

The new Visitor Centre had been conceived and promoted by Brian and was to be his crowning glory, the apogee of his career and now in his moment of triumph, fate had dealt him the cruellest hand. So was it any wonder that his head was a kaleidoscope of whirling emotions as he helped Conchita holding the single suitcase onto the back of his old motor bike. Kick starting the bike into life (*not easy wearing sandals*) he made space for Conchita before the pair of them rode out of the Reserve and into history.

**BRIAN AND CONCHITA FLEE
THE FORMBY SQUIRREL RESERVE**

IT WAS ALIENS
WHAT DONE IT

The momentous events in Formby had been reported far and wide. News crews from as far as China and Japan were besieging the now cordoned off Formby Reserve, all desperate for footage of the tree planters mechanical rampage. Helicopter hire rates had gone through the roof as news crews became evermore desperate for footage. The skies above the Resort now reverberated to the sound of whirring rotors.

After several "near misses" Air Traffic Controllers at nearby Woodvale Aerodrome, no longer able to deal with the volume of traffic, finally admitted defeat and issued a "no fly order" over the Reserve. The issuing of the "no fly order" was seized upon by conspiracy theorists as truth that the Government was trying to cover up an alien invasion. This theory enhanced by grainy photographs posted online which appeared to show giant spider-like creatures attacking cars and people in the foreground of the burnt-out Visitor Centre.

With the *no fly zone* being rigidly enforced, the Forensics team were now able to begin to recover the bodies of the unfortunates who had, in the words of a bulletin issued by the National Trust 'given their lives in the fight against coastal erosion and global warming.' Amongst these unlikely warriors listed along with their occupations were The Countess of Parbold aka Svetlana Simpkin (occupation unknown), Gino O'Riley (Hot Dog vendor), and Footo Inmoutho (World renowned Conservationist Architect).

Footo Inmoutho's death had been particularly unfortunate for the Trust, as had he lived; he would most definitely have faced charges regarding the design and lack of fire prevention for the thatched roof on the Visitor Centre. His attendance at the opening had been a last-minute decision as he had originally been booked to be the Guest Speaker at the World Pogo Stick Championship in Rhyl. An avid pogoist himself, he had hoped to show off a revolutionary new Pogo Stick made out of sustainable bamboo, but had been thwarted when Customs impounded his pole saying 'it posed a threat to native bio diversity and would have to be eradicated and quarantined for six months.'

Given the relative proximity of Rhyl to Formby he had decided to attend the opening of his creation, arriving just in time to see the Countess of Parbold being interred by the tree planter.

He died the way he lived, a conservationist to the end, trying desperately by use of the spare remote control, (dropped by Brian Betwetter as he fled), to regain control of the homicidal tree planters. Despite his best efforts he fell to a Pinus Sylvestris sapling through the heart as he tried to prevent No 4 breaking into the building. In a fitting tribute a tree would be planted on that very spot to honour his heroism.

NUTS TO THE HUMANS

What happened to the Squirrels, I hear you asking!

With the Resort cordoned off from the public, the immediate effect on the Reds of Formby was a severe nut shortage. The Reds had become totally dependent on human visitors bringing copious amounts of nuts into the Reserve and had sacrificed their own innate ability to forage for food, for a starring role in Brian Betwetter's *Fantasy Conservation Project*.

In dreys all over the Reserve angry voices were being heard. The Revernants never popular with rank and file squirrels, were now seen as the architects of the food shortage, along with their mentor the Propaganda Minister Gurballs Red. Fatally misjudging the mood of his fellow squirrels, Gurballs Red had made a speech in which he had said what had happened at the Reserve should be seen not as a disaster, but more an opportunity to return to the old ways of fortitude and self-sufficiency. This was translated by the angry mob outside the Ministry for Constant Truth as meaning "no more nuts."

Almost immediately the mob as one voice began chanting '*we want nuts, we want nuts, we want nuts*.' Gurballs Red tried to continue but was drowned out by the insistent chanting and seeing that the situation was getting out of control, he unleashed the Revernants to disperse the angry mob. This tried and tested method of crowd control had always worked in the past and Gurballs Red was fully convinced it would work again. **Big mistake**.

Among the crowd were many soldiers, veterans from the battle of Wam Dyke Bridge home on leave from the front, battle hardened and now disillusioned by the nut shortage, they were in no mood to be dispersed by baton wielding Revernants, so instead of fleeing the crowd buttressed by the soldiers, they stood their ground repulsing wave after wave of evermore desperate Revernant attacks. Skulls cracked as the now hysterical Revernants lashed out in every direction as it became clear to them they were in danger of being overwhelmed. Despite all their efforts, the sheer weight of numbers prevailed and Bhastado and his fellow Revernants battered and bitten, had no choice but to lay down their weapons and beg for their lives.

Worse was to follow as the mob buoyed by their victory poured into the Ministry in search of Gurballs Red. Finding him hiding under a gorse bush he was dragged outside to face the fury of the crowd, chants of *'kill him, kill him, kill them all,'* rained down from the trees as more and more squirrels appeared in the surrounding trees attracted by the disturbance.

To paraphrase: "cometh the hour cometh the Squirrel", or put bluntly, every mob needs a leader, and this mob's leader was Olaf Nutter the former highly decorated Commander of the Viking Division of the Red Army of Formby.

With a booming voice he stood forward to seize control of the situation,

'Let me through, let me through.'

The mob parted to allow him access to the badly beaten Revernants.

Gurballs Red seeing Olaf Nutter as his salvation tried to take control of the situation, intoned in a voice more suited to a weasel than a squirrel:

'Ah Commander just the person, there appears to have been a small misunderstanding between my men and some of the populous, perhaps you could provide us with an escort, so that we may not further provoke an already untenable situation, which without remedy could result in consequences not foreseen by either side' (*Gurballs speak for " Help"*).

'I'll escort you alright! Right to the Border you

and your thugs.'

Commander Nutter's reply was met with wild cheering from the trees:

'No Commander you misunderstand, I wish to be escorted to the Great Leader to explain to him the legitimate concerns of our fellow citizens regarding the nut shortage.'

This statement was met by a cacophony of booing and jeering and more chants of '*kill them, kill them, kill them.*'

When news of Gurballs Red's predicament was relayed to Vermillion Red it presented her with a dilemma, to intervene or not to intervene? Normally dissent of any kind would be ruthlessly suppressed, but this situation afforded her the opportunity to rid herself of her most implacable foe and rival for the leadership of the Republic. So, when Betterred suggested that the Kemel Noir be sent to rescue Gurballs Red from the mob, she said that she would have to consult the Great Leader, and as he had left instructions not to be woken, Gurballs Red would have to take his chances with the mob.

A PYRRHIC VICTORY IS STILL A VICTORY

With Kemel Red in his dotage the future of the Red Squirrel Republic had never looked so uncertain.

Despite the Reds overwhelming success at the Battle of Wam Dyke Bridge and their ruthless removal of the ruling Grey Squirrel elite by use of the chemical weapon Nuttachoc, the Republic now teetered on the brink of starvation.

The Formby Reserve had provided the Reds with food and protection and with its closure the Reds simply couldn't cope. Stripped of Brian Betwetter's shoot to kill policy, it would only be a matter of time before the Grey hoards were once more massing on the border. The Reds had thrown all their resources into maintaining their army, foraging for food had been abandoned as the visitors would bring all they needed. The idea that the Reserve would ever close had been dismissed as laughable!

Well they weren't laughing now as the closed Reserve and its now derelict Visitor

Centre took centre stage in what was labelled the"trial of the century" by the newspapers.

The National Trust had decided to sue Yokahama Mutual for their failure to honour the Trust's claim for the destruction of the Visitor Centre and the subsequent loss of life incurred by the disaster.

Yokahama Mutual were the World's largest seller of climate change insurance. They had reached this position by a ruthless policy of acquiring smaller companies that were in financial difficulties, one such company "The Yeoman of England Insurance Company" had been the National Trust's insurers since its creation in 1895.

Known by one and all as the Yeo, it had been brought to its knees by Lady Twistleford Green the octogenarian chatelaine of Dimdismal House who had conspired to burn to the ground the east wing of the house while indulging herself with an indoor barbeque. The east wing had contained an extensive art gallery which contained works by major artists such as Rubens, and Tintoretto. These works lost in the fire, had been part of the Twistleford collection bequeathed to the National Trust by the late Lord Twistleford in lieu of death duties, and were the property of the Trust who duly insured them with their long time insurers "The Yeoman of England Insurance Company," who had shared the risk with Underwriters to mitigate any possible claim, normal practice in the insurance industry and all perfectly above board!

One small problem! Due to a computer upgrade failure, the Underwriters had never been paid their premium, and now faced with a multimillion pound claim, they refused to accept any part of the claims liability, leaving it all down to the Yeo to shoulder the complete loss.

Years of losses now compounded by the loss of the Twistleford Collection forced the Yeoman of England to turn to their Bankers for an emergency fund raising, to prevent a collapse of the company. The Bankers were less than supportive but suggested that both their interests may be best served by accepting a takeover bid by Yokahama Mutual Insurance Company who just happened to be a customer of the Bank!

At the stroke of a pen, The Yeoman of England Insurance Company disappeared into history, and the Yokahama Mutual became the National Trust insurer. The relationship getting off to a rocky start by Yokahama dismissing the Trust's claim for the loss of the Twistleford Collection by virtue of the Trusts failure to take action to prevent Lady Twistleford Green from indoor barbequing, despite numerous warnings from the local fire brigade.

Despite much heated correspondence, the Yokahama stood firm. Lady Twistleford Green had been the Trusts tenant and their responsibility, and by not curbing her barbequing they had abetted her in her reckless behaviour, and this had made the Insurance Policy null and void.

On Counsels advice the Trust had had to abandon their claim against Yokahama and were now forced to meet the loss of The Twistleford Collection along with the damage caused by the fire from their already overstretched own resources.

BENVENUTI
A ROMA

Brian and Conchita had arrived at the Vatican with the smoke of the burning Visitor Centre still fresh in their nostrils. Despite the 1400 mile journey, apart from a puncture in Ostend, Brian's scooter had performed admirably well. However the journey had not been without incident, a run-in with a pack of Hell's Angels in San Marino had been deeply troubling and had caused Conchita to see Brian in a completely different light!

When told that a private audience with the Pope would not be possible as His Holiness was attending the Italy v Argentina football match, Conchita slumped to her knees and begged for Political Asylum. Father Ratsarsee the Pope's Private Secretary seeing Conchita's obvious distress, counselled her by telling her that the Vatican did not offer Political Asylum, she could however, as a Nun, apply for the Ancient Right of Sanctuary.

When Conchita heard this she was overjoyed, but her joy was tempered by caution telling the Cleric.

'But I have left the Church, I have renounced my vows,' he replied.

'Do not be afraid my daughter, as a Bride of Christ you will always be a Bride of Christ no matter what earthly conventions you may or may not have entered into.'

Brian however was a completely different case, an avowed atheist he would have to try his luck elsewhere.

With her faith fully restored and resplendent in her pristine Habit, Conchita sat in front of the video camera at a specially prepared table in the Sistine Chapel, next to her was an empty chair. Ostensibly here to record a statement for the upcoming court case between The National Trust and Yokahama Mutual, she departed from the prepared text and with a backdrop of Angels festooning the walls, Conchita delivered a withering attack on the National Trust, calling it a self-serving oligarchy, that only existed to perpetuate itself at the expense of God-fearing Christians, more concerned with sexuality than Christianity it was an anathema to the Church's teachings and represented all that was wrong with Britain today!!!

Turning to the empty chair she declared that no one exemplified this moral decay better than her one-time partner Brian Betwetter, calling him a vile seducer who had beguiled her with tales of a paradise right here on earth in the form of the Formby Squirrel Reserve. This "paradise" had turned out to be no more than patent chicanery masquerading as conservation in pursuit of profit!!

Leaning forward and staring deeply into the camera, Conchita stated, *(now returning to the supposed purpose of the video)* that the disaster in Formby had been caused by the Trusts over-arching pursuit of money, and in a bombshell moment she revealed that Brian had confided in her that he had been experiencing control problems with the robotic tree planters and had wanted to cancel their part in the opening ceremony, but had been overruled at the last minute by Ghastlena Gristle-thorpe, Chairperson Emeritus of the National Trust who had told him in no uncertain tones *'that the show must go on.'*

Concluding her Video Conchita said she would pray for the souls of the departed, and she had a special prayer that Judge Jeffreys would be guided by the hand of God in his upcoming trial deliberations.

I'VE GOTTA GET OUT OF THIS PLACE

Father Ratsarsee saw himself as a modern Christian and liked to surf the Net whenever pastoral duties would afford him the time and liked to "check out" whatever was trending. Currently the meme of the minute was … "HE TURNED MY WIMPLE INTO SOCKS."

Mildly amused by the title, he was horrified to see that the post in question related to the supposed confidential video made by Conchita, along with some additional footage where Conchita had given a no-holds barred, warts and all account of her time married to Brian.

Nothing was guaranteed to dent the Pontiffs good mood more than another sex scandal involving the church, so he made an executive decision… Conchita would be sent to Albania to continue her vocation and Brian would be given a Vatican diplomatic passport and smuggled out of the country.

Disguised as a Cardinal, Brian arrived in Ecuador

and immediately claimed political asylum. His claim was fast tracked at the behest of the Vatican and in no time at all Brian found himself working in the Galapagos Islands on a turtle conservation project, where he was known to the locals as "El Ardilla" (the Squirrel).

With Conchita safely installed in a Nunnery in Tirana the story now moved back to the High Court in London, for the "Trial of the Century".

GIVE THEM
ENOUGH ROPE

Under current circumstances, Lord Justice Jeffreys would be the last person on earth to be put in charge of such a high profile trial, but due to an outbreak of Coronavirus contracted by a panel of judges on a fact-finding mission to Wuhan, and their subsequent quarantining, Judge Jeffreys had been rushed back from suspension/gardening leave and put in charge of the National Trust versus Yokahama Mutual trial.

The suspension was a direct result of a speech he gave to the BBHC (bring back hanging campaign), in which he alluded to the fact that he was a direct descendant of the notorious seventeenth century "Hanging Judge Jeffreys" saying.

'Just because his ancestor had hanged a few Welshman didn't necessarily make him a bad person.'

Meant as a joke, it had provoked a media storm when it had been secretly recorded and posted onto the internet.

The Lord Chancellor had no choice but to discipline Judge Jeffreys by virtue of a suspension and further ordered that the judge would have to undertake a racial awareness course before he could be allowed to resume his career as a trial judge.

The course having been undertaken, and kicking his heels at home whilst serving out his suspension, Judge Jeffreys (known to his friends as Ropey), was delighted to receive a call from the Lord Chancellor's Office, and further pleased when he was appointed to the National Trust v Yokahama Mutual case. This had come about as the quarantining of so many judges had left the legal system near to collapse, and, but for his recent lapse, Judge Jeffreys had been a highly thought of Judge specialising in complex commercial trials.

HAPPY DAYS ARE NOT HERE AGAIN

As the sand dunes at Formby roamed inexorably inland, their progress now unhindered by the planting of trees as the tree planting program was now held hostage to the unfolding drama being played out in the High Court, and with the Reserve still closed to visitors things looked bleak for the Red Squirrels of Formby, who, now deprived of the nuts brought by the visitors were beginning to endure genuine hardship.

> *The days of plenty now over, the squirrels would go to bed at night hungry for the first time ever. With this hunger came unrest, dreys no longer safe from marauding gangs of their fellow citizens who rampaged into homes in an ever more desperate search for nuts.*

With the Great Leader in his dotage, and his would-be successors fighting amongst themselves like rats in a sack, a sense of hopelessness pervaded the closed Reserve.

THE TRIAL OF
THE CENTURY

Lord Justice Jeffreys refreshed by his "gardening leave" was feeling rather smug with himself, as his judicial limousine approached the High Court on day one of the National Trust v Yokahama Mutual case. He had weathered the storm and was now in charge of a major trial again.

As Lord Jeffreys car approached the rear gates of the court, it was met by the bizarre sight of protestors dressed as daffodils and leeks carrying nooses chanting *'Jeffreys is a racist, a racist, a racist, a racist.'*

As the electric gates opened and the car swept into the rear courtyard of the court, Judge Jeffreys realised, with breathtaking understatement that he may have been a little premature in assuming that the fuss about his speech had died down!

The Defendants, Yokahama Mutual Insurance Company was represented by Donal Thump QC, a brusque no-nonsense Ulsterman, who had successfully defended numerous actions brought against his clients. A ferocious cross examiner, his epithet of "The Ulster Pitbull" totally deserved, and could be testified to by the numerous witnesses that he had reduced to tears while under his remorseless attack.

The Plaintiffs were represented by Lady Elisa Billingsgate Fudge QC, a slightly built women with a big brain. Her appointment had been seen by other members of the legal profession as a big risk, as her previous experience as a specialist in transgender rights may not have prepared her for dealing with Donal Thump.

Making her opening address directly to Judge Jeffreys in a court bursting at the seams, Lady Fudge said:

'This case is not about climate change, but about a corporate behemoths failure to accept its liabilities, no more no less.'

.......then she sat down.

Judge Jeffreys looking up from under his glasses at Lady Fudge inquired.

'Is that it?'

'Yes, my Lord, I have no wish to waste the courts valuable time with some long-winded diatribe. My case requires no flowery obfuscation, I am prepared to stand by the facts.'

Now it was Donal Thumps turn.

'My Lord, the reason my learned friends' opening address was so short is because she is afraid that a more reasoned address would only expose the paucity of her position. I have no so such shortcomings and would offer my clients position thus, Yokahama Mutual Insurance inherited the debts and liabilities of the Yeomen of England when it was forced into financial difficulties by a combination of financial ineptitude and an over reliance on its long term relationship with the National Trust. This relationship was sustained by charging totally unrealistic premiums, and then arbitraging the risk to Underwriters in what can only be described as playing "Russian Roulette." Sooner or later the gun had to go off, and it did with a bang, when Twistleford Hall was destroyed by fire along with the Twistleford Art Collection. In a monumental blunder the Yeomen of England had failed to pay the Underwriters their fees and had left themselves totally liable to pay the whole claim from its own resources which it could not do. Staring ruin in the face, it was rescued when my clients, abetted by their Bankers, took on the liabilities by acquiring the Yeomen Insurance Company for one Pound, which, given the liabilities, looked like a very generous offer indeed.'

Pausing for a glass of water sipped in such a manner as to heighten the sense of theatre, Donal Thump continued.

'I will now bring you to the nub of the case and the reason for this thoroughly vexatious litigation before us today. On examining the claim made by the National Trust for the Twistleford fire, vital documents were found to be missing or destroyed. Also an attempt had been made to erase the file from the Yeomen's computer system. This failed attempt to destroy the files was only remedied by a forensic reconstruction which unearthed correspondence from the local Fire Brigade which had attended Twistleford Hall on three previous occasions prior to the disastrous fire, due to the octogenarian Lady Twistleford Green's penchant for indoor barbecuing. One particular letter from the Fire Brigade states that Lady Twistleford Green was a "fire hazard" and that she should be removed from the Hall to a place of safety immediately.'

At this point lady Elisa Billingsgate Fudge jumped to her feet shouting

'My Lord what does any of this have to do with the case before us?'

Donal Thump leapt into the attack.

'My Lord unlike my learned friend's tawdry opening statement, I would seek with your Lordships indulgence to lay before you all relevant facts, and if I am permitted to continue, it will soon become clear as to why I have laid these facts before you.'

At this point a member of the public wearing a raincoat leapt to his feet. Discarding the raincoat he revealed himself to be naked apart from a daffodil masquerading as a fig leaf covering his private parts, and almost immediately began chanting,

'Jeffreys is a racist, a racist, a racist, Jeffreys is a racist, a racist, a racist.

PROTESTER DISPLAYS 'BARE' FACTS OF THE CASE!
(ARTIST'S IMPRESSION)

Before he could launch into a third verse he was forcibly ejected from the court by Court Ushers, one of whom removed his Ceremonial Robe and by wrapping it round the naked protester thus prevented any further outrage to public decency. *(All of this being recorded by members of the public on their mobile phones).*

At this point Judge Jeffreys made the controversial decision to dispense with the public and continue the trial *in camera.*

After taking lunch, the court now having been cleared, Judge Jefferies resumed the deliberations. Indicating to Donal Thump, Judge Jeffreys sai.

'You may continue your opening statement Mr Thump.'

'Thank you my Lord,' he continued.

'Having received the Chief Fire Officers' letter recommending that Lady Twistleford Green should be removed from her grace-and-favour accommodation, as she clearly presented a danger to herself and the Hall by continuing her nocturnal pyrotechnic activities. The Trust did nothing. As to why the Trust did nothing can only be conjectured. Incompetence perhaps, or could it be the fact that Lady Twistleton Green had bequeathed to the National Trust a multi-million Pound inheritance, the only condition of this bequest was that Lady Twistleford Green be allowed to tenant the Hall for as long as she lived. This indeed would be reason not to attempt to remove the lady from the hall for the fear that she would feel aggrieved enough to cancel her bequest, thus depriving the Trust of a considerable amount of money.'

Donal Thump continued.

'When my clients Yokahama Mutual assumed the liabilities of the Yeomen of England Insurance Company, it rightly set about discharging its obligations, and its priority was dealing with a considerable backlog of outstanding claims. The largest of the claims related to Twistleford Hall and the loss of its Art Collection, and because the Yokahama has a financial obligation to its investors, the size of the claim meant it would have to be thoroughly investigated and as a result of facts unearthed and touched on earlier in my submission, the claim was denied due to the non-disclosure of Lady Twistleford Green's penchant for arson, euphemistically referred to as "*indoor barbequing.*" No insurance company on earth would insure a property against fire, when said property was inhabited by an arsonist, and by not removing Lady Twistleford from Twistleford Hall until the night of the fire, and only then by means of a Fireman's Ladder, the National Trust had clearly voided any claim it had against its insurers, my clients, Yokahama Mutual Insurance Company. The denial of the claim totally poisoned the relationship between my clients and the National Trust and sowed the seeds for today's litigation. I will show that the Trust has learned nothing from the Twistleford Hall debacle and continues with its own reckless belief that no matter how incompetently they behave *they can always rely on the Insurance money to bail them out,* and that brings me to the claim that your Lordship has been tasked with adjudicating on.'

*Judge Jeffreys now intervened to say that as to
the lateness of the hour it would be better to
continue at 10 o'clock the following day.*

Having run the gauntlet of daffodil and leek clad
protesters for a second time, and now with the
trial being held *in camera*, Judge Jeffreys opened
day two by inviting Donal Thump to continue his
opening address.

'Yokahama Insurance, unlike the National Trust,
is not a charity, and has a fiducial responsibility to
its shareholders and its employees, and in light of
that, it had no choice but to disavow the Twistleford Hall claim. Whilst sympathising with the
Trust's position, Insurance cannot be seen as a
financial "fire fighter" that will come to your rescue when you may have been complicit in starting
the fire in the first place.'

'Which brings me directly to the case before
your Lordship.'

'At last' muttered lady Billingsgate Fudge under
her breath. A virtual spectator up to now, her
tactic of not offering a more robust and detailed
account of why the Trust sought legal redress,
seemed to be backfiring in a spectacular fashion!

Donal Thump had no such concerns, as he foren-
sically ripped the National Trust's claim to pieces
with all the zeal of a latter-day evangelist, invok-

ing the name of the Lord whenever possible for maximum effect. This tactic somewhat wasted by not having a jury to play to, nonetheless seemed to be having a positive effect on Judge Jeffreys who appeared to hang on to his every word.

Had this been a boxing match the towel would have been thrown in long before the case broke for lunch!!

OUT OF THE BLUE

Having enjoyed a particularly good lunch washed down by a "Claret of distinction," and fortified by reports brought to him by his Clerk that the protesters had abandoned their protest, *(their daffodil suits offering very little protection to the now inclement weather)* Judge Jeffreys permitted himself the indulgence of thinking about his next case, already having decided that the National Trust's case was dead in the water, while further musing what on earth were the National Trust thinking appointing Elisa Billingsgate Fudge to present their position against someone like Donal Thump. Further reverie gave him the mental picture of a cannibal tucking into a female missionary, freshly served from a large cooking pot!!

His musing over, and donning his judicial robes, he was stopped in his tracks by his Clerk handing him the phone, if this was his wife asking him to pick up the dry cleaning again he would tell her *where to place said items*!

'Angharad I've told you not to bother me while I'm in the middle of trial.'

The caller in a rather brusque manner identified

himself as Peter Ribblesford Smudge the director of MI6.

'Listen Jeffreys we appear to have a bit of a situation regarding this National Trust thingy, where are we up to?'

Before he could continue he was angrily interrupted by Judge Jeffreys telling him in no uncertain manner he could not in any circumstances discuss the National Trust Case as it was subjudice. Ribblesford Smith was having none of it.

'Matters of National Security must always take precedence over procedural niceties... we need the National Trust to win.'

The now incandescent Jeffreys almost exploded.

'How dare you ask me to interfere with justice, that would be an anathema to all I stand for, I simply will not do it.'

'Ok then, you'll have to recluse yourself when tomorrow's papers publish sensational facts relating to your private life, need I say more?' replied Ribblesford Smudge.

Taking a deep breath Judge Jeffreys with a voice full of reticence replied.

'Just how will the National Trust be allowed to win, their case is pretty hopeless you know?'

Ribblesford Smudge now totally in control of the situation intoned.

'In about half an hour you will receive an offer on behalf of Yokahama Insurance Company from Donal Thump. This offer will be to pay the Trust's claim for the Visitor Centre and the subsequent damage to property but will not in any way accept liability for the deaths of the Countess of Parbold, the Japanese citizen Footo Imoutho or Gino O'Riley. These deaths having already been deemed misadventure by an Inquest Jury will have to be dealt with at some other time and are not subject to this offer. Is that clear enough for you?'

Within the allotted time frame and with the trial paused for legal arguments, Donal Thump and Elisa Billingsgate Fudge joined Judge Jeffreys in his Chambers.

Donal Thump with no hint of dissatisfaction delivered the Yokahama's offer to Elisa Billingsgate Fudge who seemed totally non-plussed, accepting it on behalf of the National Trust without comment.

Judge Jeffreys concluded the trial and reserved his judgement to a later date.

THAT WAS A
SURPRISE

When told of the outcome of the trial, Ribblesford Smudge confided in his deputy Gerrard Funk.

'That was a close one, we only just got the Americans to play ball, dammed whistle blowers, I'd shoot the lot of them if I had my way.'

'Have they traced the source of the leak?' inquired Gerrard Funk

The leak in question concerned the details of the nuclear submarine USS Maralago's covert mission to Liverpool Bay and it's testing of a revolutionary radar disruption system. An email with an attachment had been posted to the National Trust's Elisa Billingsgate Fudge by a group calling itself "Amigas de la ardilla" (friends of the squirrel). This revealed classified documents that concluded that in all probability the tree planting rampage at the National Trust's Formby Squirrel Reserve had been caused by the submarines radar beam.

'The only thing we can say with any certainty is that the email emanated from somewhere in South America, Ecuador possibly,' concluded Ribblesford Smudge.

'How did we get Yokahama to pay up, looked to me like they were winning the case all ends up,' inquired Gerrard Funk.

'Surprisingly easily as it happens. Our friends in the C.I.A mentioned the two magic words guaranteed to work on any American Company **"National Security."** Hard part was getting the National Trust to accept it. That Elisa Billingsgate Fudge is a tough cookie and wouldn't accept the settlement unless it contained a promise to re-visit the Twistleford Hall case.'

'We could do with people like her working here Gerrard. Do a background check, you know the usual thing, political affiliations, Facebook posts, who she slept with at university, that sort of thing, and while you do that I've got a call booked on the Red Phone to the Director of the C.I.A to tell him how we've pulled their" chestnuts out of the fire" yet again... can you imagine the fuss if it was revealed a fully armed American Nuclear Submarine was in the Mersey trialling a Communications Death Ray and our government knew nothing about it! Hey ho time for my Phone call.'

OPEN FOR BUSINESS ONCE MORE

The opening of the rebuilt Visitor Centre was a sombre affair. No razzmatazz, no fireworks, just a short address in which the names of the fallen were read out, followed by a minute's silence. The Ceremonial Ribbon was cut and lady Eliza Billingsgate Fudge announced to the handful of people gathered there.

'I now declare this Centre to be open.'

Initial plans for the re-opening had included a tree planting ceremony but this had been thought to be insensitive and had been abandoned.

Soon the crowds were flocking back into the Reserve, many of the Visitors would be heard to remark *just how skinny the Squirrels were looking* and wondered how they had got on during the Formby Reserve's enforced closure!!!!!

But that's another story and another book.

Printed in Poland
by Amazon Fulfillment
Poland Sp. z o.o., Wrocław

57432861R00103